Obsession

Charlotte Pickett

Contents

Inception

A pair of strong hands fisted a hold of my hair and dragged me through the floor. "Stop, it's hurt! " My mouth had dried up at the constant screaming and panting for air, as the pain-inflicting upon my scalp twice up as I struggled.

He barked " Shut up, you whōre. I'm gonna teach you a lesson. And don't you fucking dare try to run away from me again. You are my little bîtch!!! And you kept forcing me to do it in a hard way, to make you understand this simple shit,"

He dragged me along until he reached his destination. The basement... The excruciating pain in my head was eased as he shoved me inside the room roughly.

I couldn't stop myself from shaking.... fear...because I knew what was coming next. He was going to hurt me and nothing would stop him. I rushed up towards the corner of the room and shielded myself as much as I could.

I heard him unbuckling his waist belt and slowly walking toward me.

And wasting no more time. He hît me with the belt mercilessly. He hît me centering my legs and thighs, and also my arms as I desperately tried to cover it up with the hope of lessening the pain. " These parts of your body help you to run. I'll. I'll. I'll beat them till you don't want those legs"

The lashes seemed never-ending... he delivered one by one every second he paused his words.

Minutes later, I couldn't sit anymore and he was still beating me with his full force.

I collapsed to the cold floor, and the loudness of his evil laugh filled the confined room. " You are so vulnerable. You little bîtch, " He started kicking my stomach until he was so panting that he had to stop and look at me with those haunting grey eyes.

I was barely alive as I tried to turn away, to hide, to escape the burning gaze of those emotionless eyes.

"No! You don't fucking get to look away!" He didn't give me a chance to breathe and grabbed my chin harshly... just to shout me in the face. The droplets of spit flew and spread over my face, "Don't fucking test me Vivan! Open your fucking eyes!"

The painful clenching in my heart became more unbearable but the fire built up in me as I still kept my eyes shut. I hate his disgusting face.

His nails dug into my jaw and squeezed my face. It felt like my jaw was going to be crushed by his fingers.

I found myself prying my eyes open to meet a pair of glossy grey eyes. The non-existent courage I had a moment ago melted replaced by utter fear. More tears started to roll down my cheek as he kissed and licked my tears. That was what that was, always the same, helpless, useless, endless tears.

My stomach sank with disgust and shame. I was on the verge of clawing his face off me.

With a sigh of long breath, he murmured. "Delicious" Staring deep into my eyes, he mumbled, " I love you, Vivan,"

Without thinking twice, my words flew out. " I hate you so much, Micheal "

The fact my airflow was cut off within a blink by his strong hand that was recently caressing my cheek, showed my words provoked him. His eyes never left mine as I clawed at his hand. He loosened the grip just before I passed out.

I could feel the metallic taste of my own blood as he started to slap me repeatedly. I lost count and the familiar numbness took over,and slowly started to fall deep into unconsciousness. My vision was blurred and the last thing I hear was " You are mine."________________

I woke up in familiar surroundings. The room was confined with the color red, which brought up the way too familiar nausea in my stomach. From the corner of my eyes, I saw a figure sitting on a chair beside the bed, unmoving and staring at me. Micheal.

As soon as he saw me awoken, a smile was brought up to his face. He rushed towards me, kissed my forehead longingly, and showered me with wet kisses all over my cheek and face. I flinched at the stings from all over my face. It definitely was swollen.

I wanted to push him off and punched him in his face badly but I couldn't move as if I was held down by restraints. His cologne hit my sense and I felt the dizziness, the rage, but the confusion on how I instantly relaxed. The aching wouldn't go away.

I felt him kiss the corner of my mouth and pull away as he cupped my cheeks with his hands...softly. So I was looking into his eyes. I could see sorrow and remorse in his eyes, or so I thought. "I'm sorry, Vivan," he mumbled.

I sighed and closed my eyes. He was the one responsible. And here he was begging for a mumble of 'I forgive you' from me. As if he himself did not actually buy the idea of me 'forgiving him' . He's delusional.

This isn't the First time. This won't be the Last time either.

" Please, Vivan. Say something to me, baby," he voice dipped to a low one as he traced light kisses on my eyebrows.

" It's okay, baby. I know you love me," he mumbled almost to himself.

I wanted to shout 'No, I fucking hate you' and cuss him out to hell and back. But the damage in my throat protested, not able to make a sound.

"You love me, " he mumbled once more and tightened his arms," Rest for now, doll,"________________

Now it seemed that this would be a nightmare I could never get out. I was stuck with him for almost a full year if I remembered correctly. He was a lot older than me. I never knew his last name or any information.

And encountering the meaningless, inhumane tortures whenever I broke one of His rules, and occasional assaults, I was 24/7 walking on thin ice. What did I ever do to deserve this?

'Oh God, help me'

Chapter 1

The next morning. . . . . .

I was trying to sit up but my tired limbs didn't seemed to be moving anytime soon. I was squirming with almost an explode-mass in my bladder. I was still in bed, my side pressed tightly to my kîdnapper's warm body with his hands around my waist. It wasn't tight, his hand simply was heavy.

Unable to remove his heavy hand, I was getting angrier...

He stirred and pulled me face first to him with a tug. I kept struggling and pushing his hard chest as an attempt to keep a distance. The low grunt vibrated off his chest. And not to my surprise, a hand gripped my jaw and pulled me into a breathless kiss.

As usual, I didn't respond to his kiss and stayed still... refusing would be pointless anyway.

He was kissing me like there was no tomorrow. I snapped, " I need to pee. "

With a light chuckle, he pulled away and lifted his arm, I rolled and crawled out of his grip onto the floor. I wiped my mouth with my sleeves as the morning breath was making me gag.

I had to take my time inching towards the bathroom to take the mass off my stomach. I took extra time to stand up properly. The pain wasn't that much as I felt my skin was sticky, undoubtedly, he had applied me the ointment while I was passed out. Thankful that I wasn't bedridden about this time.

I hesitantly looked at my reflection in the mirror. I looked like...shit ... Useless ...he said.

My cheek was stained brown by Micheal's slaps. My eyes were puffed from crying. My skin was pale, adding up the self-conscious purple marks on my sore wrists.

I plopped down on the bathroom floor and brought up my knees to my chest, hugged them as to cope with the situation while thinking about my family.

My parents were teachers at church. We weren't in terms of wealth, but we were contented, and happy.

Which had been in my life, as the greatest gift from God was six years ago, the time I learnt my mother was pregnant and months later, a heart-melting emerald-eyed baby blessed our family with her arrival and to have her as my little sister, who was five years old by now.

To recall, I wasn't really bullied as my parents kept me on the line to earn mutual respect and so, to keep boundaries, to make friends and not enemies. Look where I was now. I should have never left the house that day... Only if I had known....

My life was damn perfect till Micheal kidnapped me.

I wanted my life back.

I wanted to go back.

I wanted to escape this hell hole.

But always ended up being caught. And faced with severe... punishment... As he said I was in 'the need of a fix.' This time was a complete waste, I didn't even get to reach the main door before I was pinned down.

My thoughts were interrupted by footsteps rustling near the bathroom.

I cried silently, 'why me?' thinking about the same question that I would never get An Answer to.

" Doll, what's wrong? " he knocked from behind the door. I tried my best not to flinch away as he entered the bathroom.

I remained silent.

He came closer and kneeled before me. Digging my nails into my forearm, I hid my face in my knees.

He was caressing my hair strands and pulled back some that were dumping on the bathroom floor.

" I'm sorry, Doll. I was so angry that you tried to escape, " he sighed.

" You can't leave me, you know that, huh?" His hand tried to touch my face but I cringed away and hid with my arm.

" Baby, look at me. I am begging you, " The desperation was evident.

'What a bipolar bastard!'

I was getting used to the pain but not his Sick Behaviors, it was just killing me from the inside.

"Doll-" he started again and tried to grab me again. I pulled away and pushed myself back against the wall wanting to disappear.

He suddenly yanked me to him and held my face harshly, earning a loud sob from me.

I wasn't ready for more of his unexpected snaps that would turn bloody... That blood won't be his.

I watched his grey eyes with hatred. I didn't think I would be able to have such hatred for a person. Flashing me one of his half-smiles, he mouthed, " Let's have breakfast, okay? "

He grabbed me so gently that he would be afraid to hurt me more and carried me outside the bathroom.

He let me sit on the bed.

Then he walked towards his huge wardrobe and began changing his dress or uniform. Maybe his work suit that he wore almost all the time except weekends.

Weekends of hellhole...he was with me all the time..

Actually, I had never been stepped outside this king-size room by myself. Instead, I was always being grabbed by my hair, out of this room by angry Micheal.

Micheal sat on the chair beside the bed and motioned me to sit on his lap, by patting his thigh.

I got up from the bed and walked towards him. As soon as I was near him, he grabbed me by my waist keeping me secured and pull me onto his lap.

Although sitting on his lap, my face was still on the height of his chest, and the muscles were poking out through his white shirt. Surely I could never beat him physically, but still, I wanted to … hurt him… I wanted to make him suffer ten folds what I had.

A kiss was placed on my temple and followed by stinging bite on my collar bone. Tears sprung up as I trembled in his hold.

As usual, someone knocked on the door. " The breakfast is ready, Sir, " the voice said.

" Come in, " Micheal said continuing with his work in distracting me with his painful nibbles in my neck.

The unfamiliar woman came in with the big tray. Well, Micheal seemed to have the fun of changing the maids.

He was straight about hurting me without a single ounce of mercy when he caught me planning about … escaping.. even when I looked like I was planning it in my mind. He showed who was in charge without wasting a second.

We ate in silence, as usual, Micheal was shoving the food down my throat though I was pleading for no more.

He never listened and insisted me on eating till he was satisfied, like always, no Choice.

After eating, the maid that was standing near the corner cleaned up the table.

"Now, off to the balcony. Go. " I cringed at the sensitivity of my ears but as soon as his words hit me, I obediently get off his lap and leaped towards the smell of fresh air.

I heard him chuckling behind me as I swung through the door and breathed in the breeze. The view up here used to crazily scared me to death because I didn't like the idea of 150 or 160 meters above the ground. But

I took my chances of trying to take in the surroundings in chances of figuring out where the hell was this place, and no luck so far.

The never-ending forest within my sight followed by few green fields, there was absolutely nothing there. I guessed this was the back yard of this mansion.

I enjoyed the breeze while it lasted.

Maybe I had been sitting out here a while because I was passed out on the cushion and woke up by a laughter that struck me like a lightning.

I hastily rubbed my eyes and looked up at the figure standing before me.

Micheal, he was facing away as he laughed into the phone. Before I could even register what he was saying, I was met with a tug on my face and soon smothered by his lips roughly sucking away the remaining of my thoughts...Everything was spinning.

" This is the real me, Vivan, you know this, " He mumbled with a strained voice.

My heart instantly sank into my stomach as I suppressed the urge the cry, I knew better not to react in this situation. One phone call, one unpredictable event, one mistake was always been the one that triggers him into a psychotic episode, especially with the stunt I pulled yesterday. He held to the ideal that I wanted to be imprisoned by him.

Micheal stared at me for so long. Like most of the times, I couldn't read the expression on his face.

He seemed to be in deep thoughts, the thoughts I wouldn't wish to find out. I felt self-conscious as he studied me. "Only you, doll," he mumbled to himself.

After a couple of minutes of just staring with emotionless gaze plastered on his face, he carried me in bridal style and set me onto the bed. His gaze promisingly warned me about going up to the balcony without his permission. Not that the door there would be unlocked anyway.

" I will be back at 5 as usual. Wait for me, " with a kiss to my temple, " will you? "

I couldn't help but stared at him as he plopped me down onto the bed... there were times like this when everything felt unreal... just how he looked good staring down at me with those stormy grey eyes and..a hint of smile tucked on his face. And how those eyes could turn emotionless with one wrong move.

After that, I prepared to study with a so-called professional teacher.

She was really professional.

Well, the meaning was I could ask her everything except assistant for helping escape.

I thought the staff, the housemaids, and the previous tutors would have a heart. I was wrong, terribly wrong.

They all would look at me horrified and scurry out of the room, once I insisted that I was being kidnapped. They would go straight out of the room.

And in the evening, the mad Micheal would barge in through the door and beat me to a pulp.

The first time he found out that I asked a maid to help me, he rushed back to the mansion from his work within an hour and whipped me drew blood and left me overnight in the Basement.

I thought I was dead, but the next morning he came by and surprised me by Apologizing to me. Weeks later and he found the butter knife I hid under the mattress.

He turned monstrous and tortured me till I blacked out. I didn't really remember what he did, sure enough, I didn't Want to Remember either.

I learned he never really Regret his actions. And I learnt to ignore it.

After two hours of studying, the tutor left and I plopped on the couch to scroll through movies that he chose for me.

He once brought me Netflix but he would go mad when I spent too much time watching through series. He controlled what I watched and I had to rewatch repeated movies, like almost, every day.

I turned off the TV and climbed on the bed to grab the blanket. Plopping on the couch again, I yawned and scooted on it.

I hoped to fall asleep faster, so I would have a space free from these, free from him, even if it's just a dream.

She knew how dangerous escape could be.

Survival took grit and courage and effort.

It was never easy to just give in either.

Chapter 2

I was awakened by a hand rubbing my cheek. It was more like poking me to wake up. I didn't need to check who it was as his minty breath fan upon my face, and his brandy cologne filled in scent.

Fluttering my eyes open, my throat was stuck with a vile, seeing the glint of his grey eyes that matched with his favourite smirk. The smirk that held the intensity, the forewarning of his unstable mood.

I knew that expression, well. He wasn't in good mood. His fingers continued to trace along my neck and the glint in his eyes dared me to move as he started to choke me with one hand, but slowly, challenging me to move away.

It became more like a familiar game status, every time would be almost the same, the same where things wouldn't end well for me.

His grip loosened on my neck, giving me the chance to breathe. Without warning, he smashed his lips to mine. The kiss was so harsh that I yelped in fear. He instantly threw me on the bed, bouncing me off.

He pushed me to the bed and straddled me. Without breaking the kiss, he locked my wrist above my head with one hand and the other handheld my nape, tightly, not giving me a slight chance to resist him.

He growled at me, noticing that I sealed my lips shut. " Baby doll, open your pretty little mouth," he said against my lips.

I stayed still, he groaned and his hand went around to grab my ass, " Want me to spank you, baby?" he chuckled darkly. Already guessing how I could end up, my brain didn't seem to work properly, I was refusing to give in.He would hurt me, anyways.

He sighed and pinched my nose, blocking my airway, and he sealed his lips with mine, trapping me. The instinct kicked in as my lungs started to hurt from lack of oxygen, and I found myself, huffing for air. He used that chance and shoved his disgusting tongue into my mouth, and bit my bottom lip, making me struggle more.

I knew what was coming. The low purrs vibrated in his chest and he dropped his saliva, making me gag.

With full strength, I was shaking with anger as I felt like I was going to vomit. I could feel his smirk as he pinched my nose again and said against my lips. "Swallow it, baby. You are mine, " he hands refusing to let me breathe properly, by pinching my nose.

I had to swallow because he seemed to determine about choking the life out of me. As if nothing happened, he got up from the bed and walked into the bathroom, and soon followed by the sound of the shower.

It took me a while to sit up properly on the bed, as I was looking forward to the clock with a dizzy head. It was already evening. I sat up and brought my knees up to my chest. I kept wiping off the tears that didn't seem to end for today.I refused to let him see my pathetic state.

Soon enough, he walked out of the bathroom with a towel around his waist, standing with his glory, my stomach churned seeing the half-smirk still sticking up to his face. His eyes still glinted, as he turned his direction towards the wardrobe to take out casual clothes. His attention turned back at me while dressing himself.

I was expecting him to throw his remarks, make me feel low, and drag the situation to blame and hurt me as usual. But he only stood there, looking out to me as if he was lost in thoughts.

'Knock knock '

He smirked and said " Come in,"

The maid came in and placed the tray on the table. "Dismissed" he said with a wave of his hand and stalked in my direction slowly. He clearly enjoyed how nervous I was at the moment.

Unable to read his expression, my head started spinning. His sick games were driving me insane. But he stopped in his trail and went around to sit on the couch. He mumbled while patting his lap two times. " Come here "

My breathing became a rugging mess, as I shakily rose from the bed to walk to him. He chuckled at my obedience. I knew I needed to make him calm.

Something was off, I could feel it. We are in silence as usual, but he didn't force me to feed him, as he watched me eat by myself. When I was full, he handed me the water and his hand rubbed my back in circles.

" It's been a long time. I think you're ready, doll. I think it's time to make a bond," he said darkly.

" Bond? " I asked nervously. I hated how my prediction was precise, I knew he was up to something.

" The tattoo," he said while shrugging like it was nothing. I was frozen, I could feel the muscles under my eyes started contracting. Then the penny dropped, I made out what he meant.

With a horrified scream, I jumped out of him and cried." No, you can't do much to me. Are you out of mind or something? You are sick! " He caught me off guard as he froze before taking his action.

But I was already backing up to run into the bathroom and locked the door before he could catch me. " Baby, open this fucking door." He banged loudly causing me to shake uncontrollably. My mind seemed to shut down due to the news I just received.

" Go away. I hate you. I hate everything you did to me," Why me? I was again asking myself the same question.Why??

" What did I ever do to you! " I cried out.

" Hmmm. You wanna play, huh?" his voice was calm and within a second the door flew open. He grabbed me by my waist and held a fist of my hair. " What did you just say?" he growled.

I didn't know where I got that courage but I spat him in the face. He wiped my saliva and pushed me against the wall with his body, harshly. The air knocked out of me as he held me between the wall and him.

" I hate you and that will be the same for the rest of my life, " I growled.

I expected him to slap me but to my horror, he chuckled and said, " I've got a wild kitten. Wanna play with me, kitty?"

"Fuck you!" I cussed him. I was sure about digging my own grave.

He smirked to give his remark, "Good choice of word,"

"Anyway, you will be bonded to me by the end of this week," he leaned in to leave a thin space between our lips," So, be prepared, Baby," he said emphasizing the word "baby".

Then he cupped my face in his palm and kissed me so hard that would leave a bruise. I fought back and pushed him hoping to leave me.

He finally pulled away and left my numb lips. He pecked me before he left the bathroom. " You should bathe, baby doll. I'm sleepy. I will wait for you in bed," he said from the outside.

I locked the bathroom door and showered as He said. After that, I changed into pyjamas.

And there that evil was asleep on the bed. I walked towards the couch and lay down there. I couldn't care about the consequences of disobeying him.He was going to tattoo me within a week.

I curled into a ball hoping I could just disappear into thin air, away from him.

Who would help me?No.Who would stop him???--------------

Chapter 3

I felt a cold thing on my thighs.I jumped from the touch because it was freezing cold and much real...

" You are such a bad girl. Aren't you? " Micheal hummed while gabbing my thighs harshly.I was struggling to open my eyes as everything seemed to be spinning.I felt nauseous.The room was lack of light indicating it was still early.

He sat down on the couch next to me and pulled me onto his lap. He had a towel wrapping around his lower region. I flinched as his wet and cosy chest was touching me.

What? Did he shower at this time?I was not sure about the time, but the temperature was quite cosy and gave off an eerie vibe, just another normal morning for me...

Suddenly he grabbed my chin and I felt him sucking on my lips,.. softly...

" I am asking you a question, "he pulled away while mumbling.

I felt sick as I recalled yesterday.But also remembered that I disobeyed him.I glared at him as hard as I could.I would fight him till the last second.

" You didn't learn. Did you? Huh?" He growled and I felt him gripping my nape." I told you to come straight to bed and you are sleeping on the couch. Do you know how much it makes me worry if I wake up without you by my side?" he said with a hint of worry near my ears and gripping my neck slowly but...painfully.

I shut my eyes so tight not to burst out into a crying mess.Then he let go of my neck and cupped my face in his palms.

" You are such a bad bad girl,""Can't you be a little nicer to your daddy? Maybe I would treat you with ice cream," he mumbled with a sinister smile while brushing his lips on mine with low purrs coming off his chest.

Could he still talk about ice cream in this situation?

" And don't worry about the tattoo. I'll be by your side, you don't have to be afraid," he said calmly.I opened my eyes and met his grey eyes.I tried to find the lie between those eyes. The seriousness in his eyes had already laced through his calm voice.

" Oh my god. You have no idea how much I love those eyes of yours," he said and pressed his lips on my eyebrow.

I couldn't help but burst out into tears.No one would help me if he was dead serious.I was doomed.I decided to make a plead. I knew his weakness. He only hated escaping.Maybe I could ask him ...nicely?

" M-Micheal, " I mumbled.

" Yes, baby. What do you want? Hungry?" he said while studying my face.

" A-Are your-really gonna t-tattoo me?" I mumbled through sobs.

I looked into his eyes with pleading eyes.He sighed and pushed me off him.I refused to give in."Micheal,"He got up from the couch and ran his hands through his hair.He looked confused.

I sat there while looking at up him.He glanced at me and cursed under his breath," Fuck,""" Damnn, why are you looking at me with those eyes? " he growled.

He walked towards me and lowered himself to my level." I'm sorry. But the deal is a deal. You can't plead me with those eyes," he said.

I was beyond furious.Why he couldn't listen to me?!I even pleaded with him??My survival instincts kicked in." Nooo! I hate you. I won't forgive you if you do such to me," I cried while pushing him as hard as I could.U nexpectedly,... he fell backwards.

I ran towards the door and tried to open the knob.To my surprise, the door wasn't locked.Who cares?

I rushed outside and ran as fast as I could along the stairs.This house no. This mansion was shitty large.

I could hear Micheal shouting my name. I felt my legs numb. I knew I made a big mistake. Trying to escape.But I couldn't care anymore.

I'd rather die than be tattooed.

I ran and ran as much as my legs carried me. It was more like ten minutes now. I was still lost.I couldn't hear Micheal's voice anymore.

I rushed towards a random room and locked the door. I looked around the room for a weapon but there was nothing.Then the window caught my attention. I checked the height to the ground. It couldn't die. For goddess sake, my body fitted that window.So I jumped.

I shut my mouth tightly and tried not to groan.It hurt like a bitch.I got up and started running for my life. I ran towards the forest and hid behind the large tree.

I caught my breath and tried to calm down.' I can't go back there. I won't .'Then I started to walk.After minutes of walking, I could see the wall and the gate. Ughh. This man was filthy rich.It was really a prison for me.

I wiped my tears and rushed towards the gate.Before I reached ten steps, a flashlight hit my eyes.Then I looked up.The gate was full of lights. What? Am I dead? Am I in heaven?

My thoughts were cut off by a voice.Shocking me to the core.

" Well, well. Look who we have here,"It was Micheal.

"Hope is the denial of reality."

Chapter 4

My legs worked like a robot tracing back the steps without even realizing it. The sweat beads started tickling down with the unsettled chill in my core.

'I'm so dead,' I never really got this so far.

My legs went immobile at the sight of Micheal pulling out a syringe, doubling up my anxiety, though the look on his face said it all, that it would not be pretty.

I froze in my spot as he walked towards me calmly, with that thing in his hand, making sure I see that clearly. I knew that I had pushed his limits.

I was debating whether to run or not as he kept his steps steadily towards me. He didn't even blink. I was debating to run as far as I could, But my brain told me that was a terrible idea. I would make it worse.

I needed to know what he was up to. Only that way would bring less harm to me. I stood up to my feet, frozen in my place. Trying to at least prepare myself in my very last moment before hell begin... But the last thing I'll be was "Ready" . Ready for the anxiety that consumed me and the fear that was inserted deep in my heart...

" Hmmm. There's no fun then. You won't run, kitten? So that ...I can chase you," he chuckled darkly.

" I'm sorry, " I mumbled. I could feel my knees giving up.

" Sorry for what?" He snapped...anger obviously lacing the words.

I looked up at him. I couldn't read his eyes. I flinched and closed my eyes as his hand reached up suddenly. I waited for the slap but it never came.

He grabbed my nape harshly with his one hand.And another hand was holding and gripping my waist painfully.

" I thought I could play some games with you.But now. You changed my mind. I'm kinda tired," he said dipping his head in my neck.

" But you made me upset, so I have to punish you," he whispered into my ears.

" Please, don't hurt me. I'm sorry," I whimpered at the harsh reality hanging around in the air.

He cupped my face and said, " Don't be afraid, kitten, you haven't seen anything, yet," he smiled.That was pretty bad. I couldn't guess what kind of smile it that. Shit.

" Under one condition," his fingers crawled at the corner my mouth, " You will learn how to kiss me back properly," he said with a low tone.

I knew it. This fucking pervert. Jerk!!!! I cursed him in my mind with every bad word I knew while looking down. " But come now. Let's get you a nice bath, Shall we?" He said while backing off from me as he simply discarded the syringe.

This man was making me insane. I weighed my chances as I glanced around. This place is more like a cluster of trees here and there, literally an abandoned castle. I couldn't see beyond the wall of gates back from the balcony because it's rarely do I have the chance to step out of that godamn confined room.

I nodded and followed him onto the car silently. He pulled me onto his lap and played with my hair on the way back...he just didn't seem to get tired of finding ways to traumatize me much a little more.

I decided to play along.... I despise this feeling of helplessness, but still, I didn't want any abuse, yet.

He grabbed my hand and led me to that room. I fucking hate this place. Pushing me into the room, planting a sloppy kiss, he chuckled," Shower now. You looked like shit. Well. Cute shit," Then he left me in the room.

My whole body relaxed in the jacuzzi as I messaged my scalp. I finished my shower and dressed up. It was morning already.

I sat on the bed and waited nervously.Actually not waiting, more like hearing for my death sentence with each second passed.

There must be a reason. I should be dead by now by angry Micheal's beatings. What was he thinking? Then I heard the door click open. I turned around and saw Micheal wearing his black pants holding the food tray, shirtless.

Every girl would be drooled over him but not me. I loathe his existence. I felt my empty stomach protesting. He set the tray on the table and walked towards me.

He stood in front of me and stared at me with an unreadable expression.. as if he zoned out.... Then he picked me up into bridal style. I felt so small against him. And I hated that to the point,I had to bite my tongue from throwing out the cuss words at him. It was fucked up already.

He sat on the couch with me on his lap as usual." I want those plump lips of yours now," he mumbled with an insane smirk on his face.

I swallowed hard and sat on his lap facing him. The faster the best. I knew that I should not make him angrier, if I loved my life, yeah?

I leaned and put my mouth onto him. I quickly tried to pull away but he pulled me by my nape and waist to hold me in place. I felt him nibbling on my lips.

" That's not the kiss. Show me what you learned from me. Suck. My. Lips. Now." He growled.

" No, let me go, no," I tried to push him. I couldn't do it. Why must he act like this every damn time???

He pulled away suddenly and smiled. " No? Hmmm," he said and pushed me off his lap while getting up.

I landed on the floor and glared at his back.

Then... I heard the unbuckling noise. Oh no. Not that. No. No. No. I felt the back of my eyes burn as my heart clenched painfully. I kept shaking my head from side to side as I chanted the word 'No'

He slowly turned around holding his waist belt.My knees gave out as he slowly folded the belt and strode towards me slowly.

" No, Micheal. Please. Don't. I'm sorry. Not this please,"I cried while clawing backwards.

" I fucking asked you for a kiss. It seems I've been too easy on you, huh?" He growled. "You have no idea how it hard is to control me from Fucking you into a coma," he laughed so loudly making me shiver.

"You know Vivan, it's hard, it's hard to work this out when you always Fuck this up!" He became more furious with each word he spoke...

Then he walked towards the drawer and pulled out the handcuff and the tape.

No. No. This can't be happening.

The memory of the first day that I was kidnapped flooded in my mind. That day I made him really pissed off. He tied me to the bed and almost beat me to death.

That day was really terrible. He almost took my innocence. But he controlled himself at that time. I was not sure how about this time.

" You made me do this, you brought this upon yourself," he said with an evil grin.

I could see his darkened eyes. Oh god. He was out of mind. I couldn't think straight. So I stood up and ran towards him and hugged his chest.

I held onto him a lost puppy as I sobbed. 'I wouldn't survive that'

I heard he dropped the belt and he said, " Babygirl?"

"It deemed stupid for not being strong enough, but what can one do when fate decides to make it a curse?"

Chapter 5

☐5."Babygirl?" I knew I would regret it later. But what choice did I ever have?

I couldn't let him do whatever he wants, at least to not let him terminate the hope that was dedicated to my freedom. He had destroyed my life, but if I just collapse, that would work in his favour.. it seemed exactly what he was trying to achieve.

I tiptoed and kissed him on the lips. I could sacrifice this. First, I needed to distract him.

One year of my life had been wasted while I had been doing nothing but cry. And he had been taunting me to the point I got comfortable in his presence Only. He was more like a toddler sometimes. He would calm down after getting what he wanted, and he made sure of getting that, one way or another.

I shut my eyes in disgust and leaned more to him. He froze for a while as he picked me up by my legs making me climb onto him. He placed me flat onto the bed never breaking the kiss. I could feel his breathing getting deeper as seconds passed.

His hands flexed painfully in my scalp as he groaned. He had again strad-dled me as he kept pinching everywhere on my body.

The ache in my legs became numb because of his weight. I squirmed under him. " M-Micheal... I-I can't b-breathe,"

But he never listened.

Then he bit my bottom lip drawing blood. The pain was unbearable. The time I felt I was in thin air, he pulled away with a big grin on his face. I sucked in my breath and pulled as much air as I could.

I could feel my own taste of blood. It was sickening. "You are such a terrible kisser," he breathed out and attacked me again.

When he finally moved away, I couldn't move from my spot. My face was burning with pure anger and disgust. He had been taunting me with physical intimation, but now, he was trying to get me cooperative.

I heard him showering...

He was humming loudly with occasional laughs.I've never seen him in such away.

I curled into the ball. I felt so vulnerable. I couldn't imagine him hurting me right now. I didn't want him anywhere near me. But he would never leave me be in peace. He would eventually find a way to hurt me, degrade me, debase my self-respect a little more.

The shower had stopped, indicating he was done, indicating he would be here at any moment.

I felt him tugging me on my waist as he set me on his lap. This agenda and routines were sickening as private as they were, just him and I, stuck in this place.

He wiped my face with a towel and held my hair in a bundle as he tugged the strands away from my face towards the back of my ears. That was so sickening...

" Hey, shhhh, "

"who is daddy's good girl? " He hummed.

"You are daddy's good girl," he hummed again as he nuzzled into my neck.

There was dead silence before he sighed intensively. " Come on. Let's eat," he said and fed me as usual.

I quietly ate the food. And he made me feed him. After that, he kissed my forehead and grabbed my chin just to stare at my face. " I have a surprise for you," He gently wiped my mouth clean with the napkin, " You're a good girl right?"

I just stared at him until he grabbed my ass, and put his lips dangerously close to mine. " Yes," I whispered against his lips.

" A reward for a good girl," he mumbled and nibbled on my bottom lip. " Are you going to behave for, daddy?"

I nodded, gulping, the firm grip of his hand on my bum wasn't helping me at all. He seems pleased, as he gave me a light pat on my bum. " Good girl," he gave me a peck before he left.

After he left, I went into the bathroom and locked the door.

I lay in the jacuzzi and lost in thoughts.' My family would think of me as a dead person. Will they miss me? Did they try finding me?'

Tears rolled down my cheeks again. That was what I had been up to...sleep, eat, cry, lay in the bathtub, and feel sorry for myself when he wasn't around.

I was here alone with a psychopath helplessly. Bipolar, arrogant, cruel man. He was getting worse day by day. I knew I was in no condition to fight against him, and no matter how it repeatedly crossed my thoughts, I could never suppress the mild panic attack coming to resurface again.

I lied there hours, I didn't know how long. The water runs cold. I felt lost. What was his next plan?? What was he planning???

A knock interrupts me... I knew that was a maid.I shouted at her, " Go away!"

" Ma'am, it's sir's order," she said nervously.

" Ughh," I groaned. I wrapped a towel around myself and stepped out of the bathroom.

There I saw a maid holding medium size box. She placed the box on the table and asked, " Anything else, ma'am?"

" No," I said coldly. I didn't hate the person I had become, because simply, I couldn't.

How could I feel extra-sorry for another beating heart, when I, myself was down in the pit? In survival mode, if I guessed it right, the manners weren't in my terms.

Patience or energy to feel such sympathy and empathy towards the individuals who turned blind eyes to my state Is Non-existent!

She vowed and stepped out. Oh yeah. She locked the door, of course.

There was a letter in the box.

"Wear the dress. As I said, I would reward you, my love. Wait for me. I'll see you around 5. I've instructed the maids to help you to prepare. I hope you will behave. Don't make daddy mad. I love you so much, baby girl. I'll take you out on a date.

P.S:: By the way, I would love to have another terrible kiss.

Daddy."

I frowned at the letter. This man...

But that was a chance. Finally a chance??? I huffed a huge intake of breath. This could be god's sign, this could be my ticket to my freedom! ' Yes, Yes, Yes!' I whispered yelled.

" You can't lock me up forever, Micheal,"---

"As she tangled the mess up in a cruel fate of arcade, win or lose, the price wouldn't be overdue."

Chapter 6

◻6.I sat on the bed wearing a beautiful fancy dress. Micheal would be here at any minute. My hands were shaking with excitement. After one year, I was going to step outside of this prison.' After the whole fucking year!'

I twisted my hands and sighed deeply. But I smiled to myself. I could smell the freedom. All I needed was to get through the main door and the outer gates that I wouldn't be able to pass by myself.

I tensed as I heard the door crack open.Micheal walked in with a usual smirk. Then he looked at me from head to toe.

" Hey, beautiful, ready?" He said while stretching his hand towards me.

I simply nodded and took his hand. He led me outside, and I took in a deep breath to remain calm. We walked towards the car. Instead of getting in the car, Micheal stopped and stood sternly in his trace, making me stop in my track.

He then turned around slowly leaning his back on the super expensive car. He folded his hands and looked me dead in the eyes. It was more like he was hesitating or debating at the back of his mind. What was he planning? He checked me out again and nodded his head slowly.

Then he sighed and opened the door for me to get in the car. He then joined with me and ordered the driver to go. He pulled me into his lap making my headrest on his chest as he gently patted my hair.

" I hope you will behave. Or there will be consequences " he said but whispered the last part. I looked up at his face. I could see his eyes darkened.

I gasped as his hands went up to my breasts. I tried to push his hands but he only chuckled and smacked my ass. " Bad girl. Don't want your daddy to touch you? Hmmm?" He bit my earlobes making me shiver in disgust.

Along the way, he was whispering how much he loved me.

I didn't pay heed to him and his words. I tried to focus on where were we. After it felt like forever, the car was pulled up at a shiny place. That was a restaurant? But it was more like a mansion.

I was admiring the decorations while Micheal was on his phone barking at someone on the line. His hands never left my waist, tugging along as he continued rumbling on the phone.

I wasn't paying attention to him. All I needed now was food. And the exist that would lead to my freedom.

We were led inside by a waitress. My stomach was in full excitement as the decorations are such a sight for me.

Maybe living in that fucking prison made me blind. Everything was new to me.

I could feel the stares and Micheal's death grip on me. He offered me a chair that was under serene lights radiating warmth, the whole place was just aesthetically pleasing to me. I cast my eyes around unable to calm my nerves.

With a cough, he interrupted my trance. He plopped his chin in his palm, his elbows supporting the budge muscle beneath his white shirt, and looked at me as if I'm the won ticket.

I snapped, "What?"

He chuckled, " You look so beautiful tonight,"

I was kinda taken back and shattered awkwardly," Thanks, umm. You look good too,"

He replied with a smirk, "I know"

Jerk! I had to admit. He was actually looking good. More like a model. But who knew. I've seen his evil side. And what he was capable of...

Was he really hoping me to forgive him back after all the things he had done to me? Because from the looks he had been offering, almost had me thinking he was finally feeling pity for me? I once thought about it and couldn't get answers.But now, I chose to ignore it. I chose my survival and not to give in... He wasn't someone to predict and contradict with.

After a while, the food was served and we ate in silence. I was peeking to and fro to make my plans of escaping. But my sane mind kept telling me that was a bad idea. I had bad feelings about this. I better be careful...

I looked around the place. Of course, there were dozen of guards.

Ignoring my instincts, I glanced at Micheal. He looked unbothered with a slight stubble resting on his eyebrows. He wasn't paying attention to me which was weird. I excused myself for the toilet. Micheal was on his phone again.

He did let me go, without further instructions. I came to realise he made a reservation, and maybe that's why he was letting me use the bathroom on my own.

I washed my face and looked at my reflection. " You can do it. Vivan, be patient. Just relax." I sucked in a sharp breath and tried to calm down.I walked out of there and sneaked up behind the waiter who walked past me.

I glanced around like one minute before entering the "staff only" room and I looked for the exist. But instead, I was lost in there. There were so many doors. It was more like ten minutes since I left him. Weird. Wasn't he looking for me?

After having mental breakdowns, I finally managed to find the door that led me to the streets.

It was already dark outside. I stepped outside and looked around. It was so quiet. I ran along the alleys. I could feel my stomach twist. Wasn't this so easy?

I took off my heels and ran with bare feet. Tears were running down my cheeks. It was more like dreaming. I kept casting glances behind my back as if someone would jump out.

" I need to find the police, "I mumbled to myself and wiped the never-ending tears. Finally, I found the police station. I rushed inside without hesitation.

I held up to the officer's hand and begged him to help.

" Miss, calm down," he was mumbling things. But I couldn't focus.

"Help me. I was being kidnapped, my name is VIVAN Kieran," I kept repeating, "Help me. Don't let him take me again,"

I didn't care if I had to hug and beg under anyone's shoes. There was no turning back."Don't worry. You are safe now," he said in a low voice.

I could see the officers staring at me and kept exchanging glances.

They gave me a blanket and put me in a room. After almost like an hour, an officer came inside the room and asked me some questions.

" His name is Micheal. I never knew his last name. I don't know where he took me," I said everything I could remember. He noted down with a nod. After that, he walked out of the room.

I could feel a panic attack rising through my throat, it was stuck and I had severe pain in my chest. I got that instinct something had wronged, terribly.

My nerves were on the end when the door was opened again, revealing the last person I would want to see.

" Well. Well. It seems my girlfriend wandered off around my city and reported me as a kidnapper."He said with a grin.

I stood frozen scaring to death.

When he made that sinister smirk, my knees gave out as I fell limp on the floor, backing away from him as much as I can.

He approached me making me burst into tears. I hid my face in the blanket with uncontrollable shaking of my body.

I expected the beatings but none came. He pulled me into a hug and lifted my chin. I squeaked out, " I- I'm sorry. I d-didn't mean to... I'm s-sorry. Please, Please. D-Don't hurt me."

My vision was blurred from the continuous tears.He tilted his head in a psychotic manner as I continuously bubbled not to hurt me. I was hyperventilating. I couldn't remember the rest till he placed me in the car and joined me.

His face lacked emotions." I think I warned you," he said coldly.

" I know. I'm sorry," I mumbled.

" You brought it upon yourself," he shot back instantly.

" What do you mean?" I asked him panicked. Gosh. Was I in his trap?

Then I noticed the car stopped. He pulled me out harshly into a building.

" Where are we going?" I asked panicked.

He remained quiet and continued to drag me into the old building, till he reached a room. There was a bedpost with women. I could see the tools. Wait a minute. Were those tattoo supplies?? It was a trap...

I started to wiggle out of his grip.

But he simply held me in bridal style and put me on that bed. I was now struggling like a wild animal. The woman held me in place and Micheal was patting my head.

" No. Micheal. Please don't. I'm sorry." I begged him.

" I gave you a chance Vivan. At first, I was trying to use the anesthetizer. But you deserve this punishment." He said with an evil grin, "I need you to be very much aware of this coming pain, a reminder for your stupidity," he spat with venom," I was expecting you to do such. It was much easier," He continued.

I was shaking with anger. Maniac!

Then the woman walked out after restraining me with the restraints. I couldn't even move. The room was silent but filled with my sobs. It was only me, Micheal, and the tattooed woman.

I tried to plead with him one last time. " Micheal, please. " I sobbed with pleading eyes.

For a split second, I thought he could have changed his mind, but as sickening as the prediction was right. He had made up his mind.

He snapped the woman to start. I cried and looked at the woman with a pleading look.

She seemed to hesitate at first but she gave me a shot, then starts to tattoo me on my shoulder. I cried and cried. I was so helpless. But Micheal seemed unaffected by my pleas. He enjoyed it!

The pain was so excruciating. I could feel my lungs deflating with the amount of screaming. I couldn't even breathe. The next thing I knew was Micheal's shoutings.

I could feel someone was shaking me to wake up. The darkness took over me, ceasing the pain at the instant.---

"Reasoning was a dirty compromise. For which he was still confused, she suffered as ever."

Chapter 7

□ 7.I woke up in a familiar room. Oh, no.

The realization hit me like a truck, ignoring the pain in my shoulder, I desperately rushed inside the bathroom and locked the door. While trying to calm my nerves, I slowly reached out to the mirror.

I found my pale self in new clothes. The pain in my chest didn't seem to fade any less as I yanked open the bandage off me. It was all sticky with dried blood with awful fresh smell. I was too angry to feel the pain.

"D.M" the cursive feature of those two letters was sitting on my shoulder as if it was mocking me, reminding me how pathetic I was. I was confused not knowing what did those initials mean?

Knock. Knock. Knock. I heard the rustlings in the room followed by the knocks on the bathroom door.

I would normally be clutching my hands on my mouth, preventing the sobs from coming, wishing he wouldn't hear me, so he would leave me alone. But I felt too numb now. I got the pang of pity for myself, staring straight back at the reflection of a girl who seemed unable to stop the tears running down her face, tainting the very little courage she had.

I gripped on my gown tightly, holding myself down from yelling out my cries.

How could he do such?

Why me?

The inchoate hope of mine quashed within a blink of an eye. This was way too much!

His raspy voice blew off the insipid courage that I never really had... "Baby doll, are you in here? How are you feeling?"

He began twisting the knob."Open the door,"

I hated him. I didn't even know whether I was resisting or waiting for a miracle to happen. "Go away!" I cried out.

"But baby, I need to know if you are okay. I was worried," He started twisting the doorknob again."Come out right now," he said with a hint of anger.

"Okay? Do you really think I would be Okay after you did such to me? You're such a moron. You coward-" I was cut off by an opening door, revealing Micheal.

Wait how did he open that-

He practically rushed towards me kissing me all over my face. I was struggling with my futile kicks.

He suddenly picked me up in a bridal style and threw me onto the bed. He hovered me with wet kisses. I stayed still. Only God will know how much I despised his touches.

To my surprise, he had connected my waist to the bedpost with a chain. The look he had on his face said it all, making my stomach unease.Why now??!! "Uh. Uh. Punishment is punishment. You tried to escape my princess," he said pulling some strands away from my forehead.

I looked at him as if he grew two heads. Can't he be serious? Can he?

" Oh god, you wouldn't know how much I missed those pretty eyes of yours," he mumbled with an insane smirk.

"You motherfucker, I fucking hate you!" I screamed in his face. His eyes narrowed at me and slowly his smirk grew bigger. I thought he would slap me but, he just chuckled and walked over to his wardrobe.

To pull out a belt.

Shaking my head furiously, I backed away slowly but failed because of trembling hands. He took slow, menacing steps towards me. I jumped out of the bed but the chain prevented me from moving furthermore.

I was on the other side of the bed while he stood holding the belt with a clenched jaw, losing his tie with buttons undone.

"Come here. Lay on your tummy now," his eyes bored into mine.

I furiously shook my head," No, you can't do such to me. Not the belt, please. I- I'm sorry. Please," I couldn't help but begged pleadingly as he held a determined look, holding the belt. But that didn't mean I would acquiesce to his inhumane tortures.

Being beaten with the belt was the worse. I knew how much he loved. He wouldn't stop once he started.

"I said now. Don't you fucking dare to test my patience!" He yelled at the last part making me flinch.

I broke down into a crying mess, sat down, and covered myself with bare hands. I couldn't run any further, he had purposefully chained me. I unconsciously slipped under the bed and pulled myself into a ball at the corner quickly.

"Tsk tsk tsk, " I heard Michael's low growls.

As expected, he easily dragged me out and threw me on the bed despite my pleas. Then he simply forced me to lay on the bed with handcuffs. "Please, don't hurt me. I beg you, Micheal, please don't hit me," I grabbed his steel-like fist that was clenching the belt as if he couldn't wait any longer.

His eyes danced with a glint as he leaned in closer. "Say daddy, say what I wanna hear, call me by my title," he mumbled brushing his lips on my cheek.

That was it. I spat his face. He didn't even bother to wipe off showing he had already known how I would respond.

"You want that huh? I see. Let's see how high your pain tolerance is," Then he started hitting my butt, back, and legs.

-swat.-swat.-swat."Didn't I tell you there will be consequences?"-swat.-sw at."I won't let you disrespect me. You are my little bitch. I own you!"-swa t.-swat.-swat."Don't fucking forget that!"-swat.-swat.-swat."Hahaha, look how pathetic you are,"-swat.-swat."Scream baby, scream. I love your little voices calling for help,"-swat.-swat.-swat.-swat.-swat.

I screamed at every lash. The force increased as he was enjoying it. My screams seemed like a piece of music to him.

"Call me daddy, now!" He screamed.

I kept silent.

-swat.-swat.-swat.-swat.

"I'm sorry. P-Please stop. I can't take it anymore,"I said between sobs.

"Then fucking call me daddy. I am your owner! Now!"He yelled while holding my face with one hand.

"No!!!" I barked him back.

Then he started ripping my clothes off my body."Say it now or I will do something that I would regret," he mumbled against my ears. Then his hands went towards my private part making me whimper.

"D-Daddy," I squeaked out.

He held my face and touched his forehead with mine. "Say it again, baby doll. Say it. Who am I?"

"D-Daddy," I whispered.

"But the punishment isn't enough, my love," he mumbled.

" No. P-Please, Please, don't hurt me. Not anymore. Please,... Daddy," I begged him.

He suddenly kissed my forehead as he spoke against my temple. "Of course, baby. You want daddy to stop?"

I nodded at him.

"Words, baby doll,"

" Yes, Daddy," I blurted out. I hated myself. But I couldn't help anymore. I didn't dare to think what he was capable of. Then he set me free from chains and pulled me onto his embrace.

"That's my girl. Shhh. It's okay. Daddy won't hurt you anymore. Daddy loves you, baby doll. Go to sleep now, I'm here. Daddy's here," he hummed to me.

He pulled the blanket onto me, kissed my head and patted cold cream on my back as he laid me on top of him.

I couldn't help but fell asleep in the arms of my kidnapper, just like always...------------------

"As fancy as 'ownership' sounds, the edge of sanity played with her illusion, incoherently crushing her soul much a little more."

Chapter 8

◻8.I could feel a hand over my head, patting soothingly, untangling my hair with a soft touch. Am I still alive? I guessed I was. The excruciating pain imploring my back proved it already.

Dry tears were on my face. The familiar pain, the feeling I would never get used to... I was laying on my stomach. Damn. I hated all these things. Why me? What did I ever do to face such?

There was Micheal, stroking my head and humming, "You brought it upon yourself, baby doll. I warned you, didn't I, "

I stayed still as I didn't have the energy to crack a sound either, leaving me no room for my smart mouth. It felt like a desert on my tongue.

I heard him sighed as he got up from the bed. My relief was short-lived as he came back just in a few minutes. I subconsciously groaned in annoyance. Son of a... Ughhh. My head hurts the most.

I felt him pulling me up by my shoulder, and that's where I groaned in pain and sent him a glare. But all he did was force a glass of water on my lips with a frown. Normally, I would take a gulp and spit it at his face.

But it was really dry inside my mouth that I compressed my anger and drank the water in all one go. Of course, I didn't miss the look of satisfaction on his smug face. I didn't realize if I was able to hate a person that much.

My hands were shaking with anger. And he observed my hands, with a frown. Did he just not do that?

That fuçking expression pretending not to know about any shit. I hated when he acted such.He couldn't be acting like a Mr.nice guy after beating me up to a pulp. But he did like he always does.

I raised a question, "Why me?"

I could feel myself shaking from restraining myself not to do something stupid. My blood started to boil and asked him again. "Why the fuck am I here to do nothing? And to tolerate all of your ill-treatments?"

There goes his infamous half-smirk as he pushed the strands off my shoulder and pulled me up to him. "Because I want you to be a good girl for me. Bad little girls should be punished by Daddy,"

" I didn't even know you. And- And you are here, torturing me whatever you want? " I asked while raising my tone.

I could see his eyes darkened. He leaned forward his head and our breaths were fanning. "Watch your smart mouth, baby girl,"

I couldn't think straight so I asked him, " What do you want??? Money??! Want to kill me? Just- Just tell me what can do to stop you doing such to me!?" I whisper-yelled.

He nuzzled into my neck and replied with a low tone almost whispering, " I want you, badly. Every damn time, even single second, it's all of yours that I want,"

His hand went down there onto my stomach through my shirt and up to my neck as he gripped on my neck, " Yes, baby, sometimes I think I want to kill you,"

I could see the glint in his eyes as he enjoyed how uncomfortable I was under his touch as his words terrified me more, "But that's not the point. I just want you to submit to me, and- "

he paused and continued, " You're just trying being a bad.. bad girl and think you could run away from me,"

" Just obey my words, baby doll. Okay?" He said running his hands through his messy hair.

That's it and I raised my tone unable to control myself. "Till when? I've been here for over one year!! And you are torturing me every single day-" I flinched as Michael growled.

"You should be thankful that I haven't taken you fully. You wouldn't know how it was hard for me to control myself from fucking you every place in this house," he growled.

I gasped and looked down, feeling super uncomfortable to face him. Why he would always turn my anger into embarrassment every single time?!!

His chuckles filled up the room making me shiver. He passed me a wet kiss on my forehead and walked out of the room with a wink.

And Locked the door...

Chapter 9

□9.I stood in front of the mirror in the bathroom and glared at the ink on my shoulder. 'D.M' My hand went up to scratch the letters on my skin till it turned red, disgusted with myself as the scratch turned into an ugly bloody piece.

I felt nauseous at the thought of him mentioning that he had a surprise for me. What would be next? Or should I say what's God's next plan for me??!

I didn't give a fuck about that too, I got the fucking tattoo without my consent. The whole fucking tattoo!!

(Evening)

I laid flat on my bed, staring at the ceiling as usual and killing the time. I heard Michael's voice behind the door yelling at someone. I didn't bother to get up from my position as I felt him approach me to place a kiss on my forehead. As usual, he headed to the bathroom.

I had slept a gargantuan amount of hours. I didn't even recognize myself as a human, being trapped like an animal for years. So I sat up lazily waiting for him to finish showering that I could at least pretend to be eager about the bullshits he would talk, that could turn into a bloody shit in a minute.

I just got used to it...

After a while, Micheal stepped out with a towel around his waist. Water drops were dripping down his bare chest, as I bored my eyes on his muscles.

I hate him.

"Are you done eye-fucking me? " He chuckled.

I sighed and turned away from him. I was just too exhausted to argue with him, like always he would win.

He sat on the couch opposite to me and mumbled, " I have a surprise for you, "

I raised a brow with a bored expression. Then he changed into casual attire, stood in front of me, motioned me to get up with an amused expression on his face.

I got up as he dragged me by my hand. And there, he led me outside of the room. Oh, finally, I got to breathe some fresh air again. I got excited as he didn't stop till he reached the main door. I realized he was letting me out of this place!!

He led me to his Ferrari and drove off. He would glance at me from time to time though he was driving but he didn't say a word. My curiosity was killing me from the inside. So I mouthed, "Where are you taking me?"

Silence.....

He still focused on the road completely ignoring me with a smirk. Oh, god. How much I want to scratch that face. But I knew, angry Michael would be more powerful than angry Vivan.

After it felt like two hours, he pulled over at a place. I was exhausted completely but as soon as I took a look at the house, I freaked out. I would say mansion.

I didn't even realize till Michael was holding my waist from the back. "Home sweet home," he said and kissed my temple with a smile, a real smile. He looked good with a smile, I must say.

But I exposed myself with a bored face. He chuckled at my reaction and pulled me inside. More than a dozen maids were standing in a line and greeted us.

"You're the queen, you're in charge," he whispered into my ears and kissed my cheek in front of them. I felt so embarrassed that my ears started itching at a point.

Then he grabbed my chin and kissed me forcefully. Touching me wherever he wanted in front of people was really an uncomfortable thing. He didn't break the kiss.

"Stop, Ca- Can't breathe," I tried to push him.

But instead, he broke the kiss, threw me onto his shoulders, and carried me upstairs. I looked down in embarrassment as I was sure the maids would see it. I didn't protest because it would be useless.

He laid me on a soft mattress and hovered me with wet kisses. I lay there, as usual, staring at the ceiling, tears streaming down my face.

No one, no one had touched me in such a way. Michael was here, over me, crushing down my ego and pride and I couldn't even protest. This had been going this way ever since I could remember.

His hands were squeezing my hands, breasts, forearms, butt and thighs while trying to shove his disgusting tongue into my mouth. He would pinch me every time I refused to open it.

He pulled away with a peck and wiped my tears gently. "Beautiful," he whispered while looking down at me. Then he walked out leaving me alone in the room but not before saying I could tour the house.

I wandered around the mansion including the amazing backyard, filled with lily flowers. He knew I loved lilies. But...I never did give him this information...

I ran through the grasses with bare feet. I felt overjoyed, confident, and relieved. And the fact there are no walls, not even a fence around the mansion made me happy.

This was an isolated palace with never-ending green fields in eyesight.

I laid there till the sun sank while relaxing my back on the ground. I didn't even realize I fell asleep till I woke up on Michael's arms carrying me in bridal style.

I felt some sort of relief. Finally, he let me outside of that prison. Should I be thankful to him? No!? I mentally cursed at myself. He's the one who caused all of this.

I stayed still as he carried me into the bathroom. Wait, bathroom? I looked up at his stoic face. I smelled something brandy. Wait, was he drunk??He ran the warm water and started undressing.

"What are you doing?" I blurted out.

"Take off your clothes," he said while roaming his eyes over my body.

"No, are you out of your mind!?" I said angrily while covering myself with my hands.

He raised a brow in a challenging manner. I tried to run out of the bathroom but he grabbed my waist easily and pinned me into the wall forcefully.

He inhaled my neck and mumbled, " I've given what you want. I took you here. Now, don't you wanna do a favour for Daddy, huh?"

I shooked my head furiously, with trembling nerves, I blurted out, "You're drunk"

I could sense he froze. He groaned and left me in the bathroom alone but not before saying to shower quickly.

I showered quickly and peeked inside the room. There he was sitting on the bed with his head hanging low. I rushed out towards the wardrobe as quietly as I can.

I could feel his burning stare on my back. I rushed to put the sweater I could grab, but the harsh tuck on my scalp sent me backwards as I fall on my butt.

The sweater in my hand was gone. His grip on that piece of cloth had me hanging on the edge with the look he was giving.

" Get on the bed, " he gritted.

"No," I whimpered.

He simply strides towards me and picks me up by my armpits.

"Shut the fuck up and don't fucking move," he bounced me onto the bed and started at me with his jaws clenched. I was holding onto the robe I have on me. But to my horror, I saw him pulling out the belt.

I stared at him bewildered readying to beg to not hit me.

I could see his eyes soften a bit, "Shh. It's okay. Just don't move," he soothes and started pulling down my robe.

I shooked my head and tried to push him. He growled, " Last warning, Vivan, "

I tried to cover myself but he was striding me. Effects of alcohol made him blind to my cries. He ripped off my robe leaving my chest bare. He pinned down my wrists over my head with one hand as he sucked in a breath looking down at me.

A weird sensation was chilling inside my chest, as I felt his lips attached to my nipple. His lip was so soft, sucking and teasing with his tongue. I couldn't help but moan. I could feel him smirking against my skin.

The realization hit me. Dammit, Vivan. He's your captor. Kick his ass. I tried to struggle but it seemed to make him angry that he slapped me hard. Tears streaming down my cheeks again.

"I hate you," I whispered and...He just smirked at me.

"Why? Why the fuck me!? You can get anyone you want!" I cried with my face turned aside.

"Because I own you, my doll. The day I laid my eyes on you, you were destined to be mine," He whispered while gripping my chin to turn my face, exposing my neck in a vulnerable position.

Then he started biting my neck and shoulder. Not soft ones, more like punishment. As if he was wanting to rip my skin off.

Oh   god.   When   would   this   hell
end???____

"On the contrary of hell, it held eight varieties and she was yet swelling on the surface,"

Chapter 10

◻10.Low growls were vibrating from his chest as he eyed my shoulder. He had already straddled me while gawking me like a hawk. His fingers tapped along my shoulder where the tattoo was, making me wince as his touch burnt the scratch. My chest was bare and exposed to his eyes.

His eyes visibly darkened as he suddenly gripped my chin and forced me to look into his eyes.

"Why did you hurt yourself?" He said lowly with a grit.

"Because I hate myself. You made me feel filthy," I said with venom that made him grip my jaw to the point I had tears welled up.

He growled and got up from me suddenly. He walked out of the room but not before saying, "If you ever hurt yourself again, I will make sure your family and the rest of the people you loved will suffer,"

He tilted his head slightly and confirmed, " And, Vivan, trust me, I won't hesitate,"

I ran into the closet and dressed myself up. I plopped down in the corner and leaned into the wall with burdens and guilt in my heart...

I was a threat to their safety.

(The next morning)

I wandered around the place, studying the exquisite designs of the interior, but Micheal was nowhere to be seen.

I strolled down into the hallway and I ended up in the kitchen, a busy one. They scurry around the corner and bowed down to me. A maid handed me a tray of toast and bacon. I grabbed it and threw it onto the floor as his words flooded in my brain, " Your family and the rest of the people you loved will suffer,"

All of the maids in the room didn't seem to care about that. They quickly cleaned it and placed another tray on the table. But one of the maids again handed me the piece of paper.

I glared at the poor girl who was no more than 25, with the venom. They were all the same. Lap-dogs and lap-bitches, serving a lunatic bastard. My glare had proven her to back off as she scurried away.

"I'll be back soon, my love. Don't forget to take your meals regularly, you know, Daddy doesn't treat well to bad girls... And I hope you understand the depth of our last conversation, so, my smart doll, it's up to you, BE A Good Girl, I prepared a phone for you, so I could check if you're okay, I'll be back after a week. I love you so much.

Daddy. . ."

I stiffly sat there on a chair as I slowly tore the letter into pieces. "I hate you. I always will,"

Three days later...

I tried to talk with maids in these three days while Micheal was away. But they would ignore me if I wasn't even there. It wasn't their fault either, it wasn't mine either, it's just their fear of being caught about helping me in a way of trying to leave this place.

Whenever Michael called directly to me, I would hang up. But couldn't avoid it because those annoying maids were holding me in place and made me face the camera. And the excruciating fact, they would follow me everywhere I go. Fuck this life!

On the fourth day,...

I sneaked out into the garden because I was tired of seeing the maids' emotionless faces. I just needed some alone time.

I was laying down on the grass with a fresh breeze, I just couldn't get enough of the sun shining above even if was burning through my flesh.

Then I heard, a car pulled back into the backyard. I stood up quickly and peaked from the bushes. And there I saw a beautiful blonde girl with a pure face coming out of the car. She was gorgeous, I must say. She seemed to be in her 30s. But I thought she was similar to someone. Michael?

Michael's sister (Lizzy Martin)

My breath hitched not because she turned in my direction but because I saw maids with horrified faces at the main door.

Why did they seem so terrified as if seeing a ghost?

But I stood there frozen because that beautiful girl was now walking towards me with a smile tugged on her face. Shit.

I stumbled back unconsciously. Double shit.I couldn't control myself, why I was shaking?

She frowned as she saw my terrified expression.

She was about ten feet away from me. My throat was dry. I didn't like the look of her staring at me with... excitement. What was wrong with me?

Then she mumbled lowly with a smile, " Hey there, cutie, are you okay?"

Then she started to approach me. I couldn't control myself so I started crying. Why? Why I was so afraid of her approach to me? I ran towards the bushes and pulled my knees to my chest.

I felt so cold. I was so afraid. I needed Micheal. What? I don't know. I needed him to hug and soothe me. I was losing my mind. I looked at her and saw she was calling out for the maids. I could hear her shoutings turned into heated whispers as if threatening whoever she was talking to.

Her frown turned into a sad and concerned expression as she turned towards me.

"Hey shhh, it's okay. I won't hurt you," she said with a warm smile. But I could see she was approaching me.

I started to suffocate. I couldn't breathe. I didn't like the attention she was giving to me. Please just ignore me. "Please, leave me alone," I squeaked out.

She sighed deeply and said, " Okay, but you have to come inside with the maids. Okay, honey?"

I looked at her with wide eyes. I couldn't trust her. Then I saw she walked into the house. The maids rushed towards me and took me along with them.

Inside, she was sitting on the sofa. I didn't even dare to spare a glance in her direction.

Within a blink, I sprinted upstairs as I ran towards my room and locked the door.

I must hide. Where do I hide???

I could hear the phone ringing. I couldn't reach there. It was more like ten times now. Finally, I could reach and answered,

"Vivan? Listen-"

I was so relieved and overwhelmed with fuzzy feelings inside my chest to hear his voice. That I cut him off. "M-Michael, I'm scared. T-There is someone out there," I cried desperately.

" Shh. I'm on my way. Now, all you have to do is to lock the door and stay in the room. Okay?" He said.

"No, I-I need you here. Right now. I-I can't breathe. W-What's happening to me?" I whined.

"Hey, listen. I'll tell the maid to give you medicine. You have to take that. Okay?" His voice was soothing but not about what he was saying me to do. I'd never take those so-called medicines, that burnt my mouth with inhumane bitterness.

"No," I squeaked out and hung up.

Ughhh. I hated medicines. Even the sight of those tablets made me vomit. I couldn't take medication instead Micheal usually forced me to take or he would inject me.

Then I heard the knock at the door with that woman's voice. I could hear the maids were protesting her. I could hear her serious voice yelling at the maids demanding to know who was I.

I didn't want to know anything anymore. I felt safe inside this locked room. I needed rest. I felt dizzy. I lay in the bed and let the darkness take over me.

"Even in the deep slumber, her soul would still be trapped in an appalling dread of an incubus nightmare."

Chapter 11

1 ^{1.}

I could feel a hand rubbing my head softly. It felt so good.. . Micheal???? I struggled to open my eyes but soon, the sight made me choke.

It was her. That lady...

Tears filled my eyes as I froze in my position. I couldn't move. She suddenly removed her hand off me in a surrendering manner and said "Hey, are you okay?"

I couldn't answer. I stared into her grey eyes reminded me of Micheal. But I could see sadness and concern in her eyes, unlike Micheal's stormy and psychotic ones.

She slowly back off as I stared at her bewildered while struggling to breathe. " Downstairs, okay??" she sighed deeply and walked out of the room.

I sat up quickly as I pulled the duvet on me. How did she even get inside??? I mentally growled along with my stomach. I peaked out of the room through the hallway. I called out one of the maids to bring me breakfast but none of them responded to me.

I plopped myself in the corner for an hour but I couldn't help anymore that I had to come downstairs to meet that gorgeous lady with a newspaper in her hands, sitting gracefully. I hugged the door frame and peaked at her.

She didn't glance at me but she said," Come sit, aren't you hungry?" I sat at the opposite side of the table about ten feet away from her. I felt a bit more comfortable because she didn't spare me a glance...

I munched the bacon and vegetables in front of me while observing her details. Her features were really similar to Michael. She just kept looking at her newspaper. That made me feel a lot better...

"Why are you here for?" She mumbled while sipping her tea calmly.

Why am I here?? I didn't get to know...

I looked down at my lap. I remembered Micheal warned me about bubbling information without thinking. I better shut up about everything. So I answered quietly, "I don't know,"

"How long have you known my brother?" she mumbled while staring at her newspaper without a glance in my direction.

I debated whether to answer or not... The instincts said "no" but I actually wanted to believe she meant no harm to me.

"I'm ...umm... I don't know..." Tears started to blurr my vision with the chills wrapped around my body. I can't... I don't remember?

"um..I been ... a year," I answered but regretted it because it seemed to catch her attention that she looked up at me with an unknown expression. Sadness, concern, anger?

"I ... think... may- maybe two..." I swallowed hard and I felt more tears spilling out with each second. God. What is going on with me?

" What? Did he-" she asked but was interrupted by a loud bang at the front door, making me jump.

I could hear Michael's voice at the front door, "Open this fucking door right now!!!"

I could feel myself shaking. I looked up at her face. Her features distorted along with a harsh breathing pattern. She was angry. And she seemed trying to calm down.

Her attention was on me. It had my stomach twisting in pain.

"Answer me, sweety. What did he do to you?" She asked. But I couldn't crack a voice. I lost my voice. I didn't like the attention she was giving to me.

Then I heard the door break down and angry Michael rushed towards us. But the lady was quick enough to grab me and placed me behind her back, as she stood in front of me. The two maids were holding me in place facing furious Michael from afar.

Then the lady said, "Damien, mind you explain THIS to me? What do you think you are doing?!"

Damien? Did she just call him Damien?

Michael said with gritted teeth, " Go upstairs, Vivan,-" he said in a low tone without sparing me a glance. "now,"

I could feel the maids were slowly releasing their grip on me as Michael glared at them. I tried to run upstairs but the lady shouted, "No one is going anywhere!!!"

I whimpered and started to shake uncontrollably. I could sense it like it was about to devour whole room... Michael's anger. And the lady was fuming. The tension was too thick. I made a quick run but the lady was fast enough to grab me and pull me into a warm embrace as I had to run past her.

It's warm. It's soft. She reminded me of my mother. She held the back of my head with one hand placing under her chin and the other hand rubbing my back. I realized how tall she was.

But the realization hit me. Last summer, I hugged one of the maids and Michael, he- he beat me unconscious because he misunderstood the situation.

The memory flooded in my head. I didn't want Angry Micheal. An-and he said he would hurt my family.

I tried to wiggle out but no use. The back of my eyes burned as I panicked... because I could feel it...his gaze.

He would surely beat me to death after this.

I could see nothing. I was too exhausted. I was tired. I just want a break.

Please leave me alone.

Please, just let me be.

"Mostly, she was tired of her own confusion about unanswered questions."

Chapter 12

----

1 ^{2.}

Mom?

Dad?

Where am I?

My eyelids felt heavier than ever. It was so cold. I sat up trying to see where I was.

I could see someone standing. Their back was facing me. My eyes wavered the more I tried to make out the sight.

"Hello?" my tongue felt heavy. I asked but no answer. The person turned around.

Mom? Mom!?

I ran towards her but she disappeared into thin air. Her voice resonating like a chill air in the winter morning." Vivan, where are you? Come back to us."

Mom? I broke down. I looked up as I saw someone standing Infront of me again. Dad? I tried to pull him into a hug but he also slipped away through my hands. What was happening???

"Vivan, Vivan, Vivan, Vivan, Vivan," those words are ringing in my head to the point it became unbearable.

And there, a few steps away from me, mom and dad were standing....holding out a hand for me. I rushed towards them but before I almost touch their hands, someone grabbed me from behind.

I struggled but my limbs felt useless nothing but a boneless appendixes. I looked up to see...him.

It was Micheal.

I felt lightheaded staring up at him with a sinister smirk, veins were popping out of his forehead.

He suddenly tugged me to the ground, straddled me, and choked me. "You pathetic little bitch, all you know is to cry and give up. You're worthless. I will make sure everyone you loved will suffer," he laughed out and pulled out a gun.

He shot them down one by one. No. No.

"No, please don't. No!!!!!!!!" "No. No. No. Please. Don't. Ahhhh," I screamed at top of my lungs.

I was on the bed in my room. I felt my heartache again, it was been a while since the last panic attack. I tried applying pressure on my chest hoping to lessen the pain.

I walked out of the room slowly. I heard voices downstairs. It was like a woman's shoutings. I leaned my head on the wall and tried to make out the words.

"Are you out of mind?! Why is this happening?!" I recognized the voice of that lady.

"Just ignore like you always do, Lizzy. I stay out of your shit, and you stay out of mine," Michael's voice was calm.

"Can't you see it?! She's frightened. I'm sure you're lying about her. This isn't helping that poor little girl. Now tell me what did you do to her and what will you do to her?!" She yelled.

"I've said! I. Love. Her." I heard him seething.

"She is just a little girl. I know it took some time to push someone into such insanity. Oh my god. So, you brought while she's in her teen years, oh gosh!!" The lady was yelling. I peaked at them in the dining room. Michael was sitting there.

He seemed to be confused. "You don't know. I- I can't let her go. "

He released a heavy sigh, "I can't live without her,"

" This is all wrong, Damien. All of this is wrong. Mom would not want to see you becoming a monster like this. I understand you had to go through all of those by yourself. And I'm sorry that I ran away. But I'm here, Damien. So please, let the poor girl go. You're breaking her, " her voice broke at the end.

It seemed to catch his attention.

The infamous smirk... again. Oh gosh. That could not be good.

" Yes, you. You ran away leaving me with that fucker alone, your so-called dad. He's dead. Look at me now, I'm nothing but someone you and your pathetic excuses can't mess with, " he rose up from his seat and towered over that lady.

" I serve no one but me! I own her and I will do whatever I want with her! She is My Godamn Property!!!" He yelled the last part.

I put my legs together to ease the tension but it didn't seem to relieve the pressure between my legs. I quickly strapped my hands to stop from wetting myself all over.

I quietly sat down by the top of stairs as I took deep breaths.

" Fine, I'll take her with me," I heard her sneering. She wasn't afraid of him...

" No, you're not. I'm done with your shit. I won't tolerate you even if you're the pathetic excuse of a sister," He growled.

The atmosphere was so intense.

I leaned my head against the railing, completely freaked out. The silence was eating me alive.

But my instincts told me to try to believe that nice lady. Maybe she could help me out of this hell. Away from Micheal.

But my family, they would be in danger then.

I tried to sneak backwards towards upstairs but at the very first step, I clumsily bumped the vase. I swore it was merely sounded. My breath hitched as I heard Michael's harsh voice, "Come here, Vivan,"

Not wanting to make him angry further, I exposed him from my spot and walked towards him with a down head.

He gestured me to come quickly. Once I was near, he grabbed and placed me on his lap.

I looked up that lady's direction, she was in tears and she seemed frustrated.

"Damien, I turned blind eyes with the guilt for you to do whatever you want. But this- this is too much. Can't you see what you have become? You became like him, just like father!" She whispered yelled and Damien visibly tensed at her last part.

"Enough!!! I'm nothing like him. I. Love. Her" Micheal yelled back while grabbing my face harshly to face her.

"I love her and I won't kill myself over a woman like a coward. I will break her and I will do as I please," he growled painfully holding my chin.

I looked at her pleadingly. She was making the situation worse.

"Damien, please. Let's start this all over again. Granny wants to see you so badly. And she- " she said but cut off by angry Michael smashing his fist on the table.

" Don't you.. fucking dare! Now get out of here before I call your precious little husband to fetch your ass," Micheal spat with such venom.

"Or you can ask her by yourself,-" He turned my face to him as his breath fanned upon my face, " See if she wanna go with you," Micheal spit out the words with an increasingly tight grip on my jaw, making me want to dug a hole there on the ground and die.

She didn't seem to be affected by Michael's words. " Honey, you don't wanna be here...right? Come with me," she said while smiling as if almost confronting a little child.

I stared at a wall and tried to ignore her.

" Go ahead, you only wanna be with me. With Daddy? Hmm? Say that you won't leave me," he hushed.

" Come with me. I can get you out of here. Okay, sweety?" she held up her hands.

"Tell. Her. To. Leave." his hot breath fanned against my cheek.

Should I? Would she help me? 'No. Don't be stupid.'

" I'm waiting..." Micheal whispered to me again. His voice hinted...the consequences.

I started to shake as I sobbed " Please, leave,"

Michael holds the back of my head and places my head in the crook of his neck. "You heard her. She's not coming with you," Micheal said calmly. Michael was drawing circles on my back, a hand was rubbing my arms.

The lady was about to say something but a loud," Bang!!!!!" went off making me jump.

A gunshot?!!!--

" Only if she knew Slashing blood with humiliation over Shedding tears with frustration was a trapped option,"

Chapter 13

1³·

I clutched into Micheal's shirt while he just sat there calmly with me on his lap. He silenced the buzzing phone with a "let them in," There was a dreadful silence as I uncomfortably shifted on his lap.

Then I heard multiple footsteps. "Lizz, Lizz where are you?!" The man's voice resonated through the hallway. Did he mean Lizzy? The lady in front of me?

"Honey, you need to come with me. But trust me, I won't ever hurt you. Trust me. I will protect you," the lady said breathlessly.

I wanted to get out of Micheal's grip and ran towards her. It was more like just a chance lighting up at the end of a tunnel. A tunnel in which I got lost and trapped in the most bloody ways, as I never really succeed in catching the light at the end, just like the escaping plans which always failed miserably. I didn't want to be in his grasps anymore...

But... But my family, they would be in danger, ...because of me??? I looked down at the floor while Micheal was sitting calmly while patting my head as if he was all aware of my storming thoughts.

The kitchen door was burst open and about ten men walked in. And another ten men walked in. They are aiming with guns towards each other.

Then a man with blonde hair who was aiming a gun towards Micheal muttered, "Lizzy, come here. Now,"

"But the girl-" She started but the man cut her words off.

"Lizzy, come here. She'll be okay," he muttered again.

"No, I can't leave her with him. Can't you see? He's completely out of mind," she whispered yelled.

"I know, Lizz,-" He paused looking at me and then Micheal with an un-pleasing look, " But this isn't the good time," the blonde guy said while never taking his eyes off Micheal.

Then more people came in rushing around to aim the guns at the blonde guy's men. I swallowed hard. They were obviously outnumbered..."I'll count to ten," Michael said with a bored expression while holding my body against his tightly as I tensed up.

Then he started counting," Ten,"

"Come on, Lizz. I promise we will get her back," the blonde guy said.

" Nine " Micheal smirked.

"I'm not leaving without the girl, Sam," that lady, Lizzy, said. So the blonde guy was Sam?

" Eight," Micheal smirked.

" Seven "

" Six "

The blonde guy, Sam, signalled his men. They reluctantly rushed towards Lizzy and dragged her out.

"Five, " I could hear Lizzy's protests.

" Four," the guys in the room were backing up. I felt a pang of fear in my heart.

" Three, "I felt remorse for not being able to tell her that I wanna come with her. That Sam guy was still standing there aiming the gun at Micheal. But he left after glancing at me.

" Two, hmmm" Micheal hummed near my ear. "Stay here. Don't move," he said harshly.

Then he got up, pulled out his gun, and walked out. I was nervous...I was confused...What if?-...

Without thinking further, I quickly followed him. I could see the blonde guy, Sam near the gates. Michael was aiming the gun at his back. Oh no.

" Ka-boom " he smirked.

A scream erupted from me as the loud bang went off again.

Did he kill him? I froze there as I could see barrel of gun jump, the next second Sam struggling to breathe on the ground.

I was just frozen like a statue. I felt like it was my fault. It happened again, now...Someone had to die because of me???

Michael slowly walked towards him and stepped on his back where the gunshot was. Sam groaned in pain.

Michael was smirking like a mad man. Lizzy ran towards Sam and pushed Micheal aside. She screamed holding on to him. She looked devastated as if it was an unexpected thing for Micheal to do.

It was like in slow motion as Micheal started reloading his handgun...I decided to do it today...To run, run like my life depends on it, but run towards him, run not to save myself but to save the blonde guy. No one deserves to die. Not today.

I pulled Michael's shirt and scratched his face as hard as I could. He stumbled back and I snatched the gun from his hand. I aimed the gun at him. Shit.

The shitty gun was heavy as hell.

"Don't move," I mumbled. I was losing my mind. Thousands of emotions and thoughts ran through my mind as his men had automatically aimed their guns at me.

If I killed him now, I'll get my freedom back but I will become a murderer. And his gang will slaughter me.

No. I can't.

But I will threaten him." Let them go," I stated shakily while he remained unaffected.

I waited as the man with Sam guy helped them to get to the car. Lizzy sent me an apologetic glance.

And of course, Michael's lapdogs were surrounding me with guns. But they backed off as Michael snapped a hand, signaling them.

I nervously swallowed as he pulled out a pack of cigarettes and started smoking out of nowhere.

The gun started to get really heavy as I stood firmly.

" Didn't I tell you not to move, Vivan? " He blew out smokes and waited for my answer till the cigarette was crushed under his shiny looking boots.

This man was sick. Now, he was being aimed by a gun and still talking about him ordering me not to move? Or he was making a fuss about my disobedience? I was panting. I backed off as he stepped closer.

"Shoot me then your little family...." He grinned with a sadistic smile. Oh god. Not again.

"No!!" I whisper-yelled.

My arms became weak. Before I couldn't register what was happening Michael snatched the gun from me and slapped me hard enough to fall back on the ground. This- That was hurt like a bitch. Stars blurred my vision.

Then the sharp pain in my neck was followed by darkness.

"You're in so much trouble, my love," my ears were buzzing with his threat-lacing laughter.

"The immaturity coating the heart of a broken man poisoned his own existence."

Chapter 14

----

(14)

I jerked my eyes open as the cold water hit my face. It was freezing cold and the pounding in my head ached my insides.

"Wake up. I can't wait anymore," a voice rasped.

It was hard to keep my eyes steady to see clearly, as the place only has a dim light that brought out a nauseous feeling. I found myself being tied to a chair. And there someone was surfing things on the table about ten feet away from me. I could barely see his back. The light was so dim that it started to hurt my eyes from trying so hard to focus. Micheal???

My throat was dry and I was shaking because this place was freaking cold and I was being splashed with water a minute ago. He turned on the lights making me shrink back as much as I can.

I didn't dare to crack a voice.

The way he was calming already scared the shit out of me. It felt like forever when he finally turned around.

Michael wearing spectacles?? I've never seen him with spectacles. I narrowed my eyes to focus but his eyes were so distracting. Something wasn't normal.

He didn't look at me instead he walked up to me with a syringe. I flinched at the sight of the syringe. Unwanted tears started to form again. I cried out as he held my arm and lifted my sleeve for injection. I struggled like a wild animal. No. Not the needle. Not the fucking needle!

"Shhh. This will ease the pain," he mumbled softly but I noticed the change in his voice, which I shook off and didn't care either...

Why? Was I a useless toy to do whatever he wanted? I turned away from him as I didn't want to see his face and all of suddenly feeling vulnerable for everything... Why was I so weak?? I got no say in all of this???

A voice boomed, " Everything ready?" Wasn't it,... Micheal???

What? But he was here. I looked up at the guy in front of me. He made a face but quickly go away and be replaced by an emotionless one.

Was I dreaming? Then a guy emerged from the dark making my breath hitched, Michael.

They were twins?! Twins?! My mouth hangs open. What on earth!!!

" Vivan, meet my brother, Daniel." He said with monotone. What the actual fuck! They got almost the exact same voice.

"Well, then, I'll catch up with you later," that Daniel guy said to Michael and he walked away into darkness leaving me alone with Michael.

The real Michael.

He and his twin got real identical features but not the eyes.

Michael pulled the chair in Infront of me and sat down seemed amused." You know? You're the cutest thing I have ever seen,-" His hands reached out for my cheek which I flinched immediately,

"- The very first second I saw you, the fate has written, I knew you are meant to be with me," he said calmly.

"But, you. You keep defying me. Just- Just obeying my words for your own good??? " He said while cocking his head to the sideway, making me whimper.

I already knew where this was leading...

"You disrespected me. And most importantly, you stopped me from killing that fucker. What's so important about him, huh!!!!??? " He suddenly becomes furious mentioning Sam, the blonde guy.

He grabbed my jaw so harshly making me wince in pain. " What? Are you falling in love with him, already?! Speak, you whore! " He shouted.

I squeezed my eyes shut. I knew that I was fucked up now. Michael was a jealous freak without a claim over my soul. He almost choke me to death when I shouted to him that I had a boyfriend...I wasn't thinking straight at that time...Which I ended up in an unconscious state with a broken arm...

He growled and yanked a fist of my hair making me scream." You ungrateful whore!!! " He was slapping me so hard that I could taste my blood.

"Fucking answer me," he yelled. But I didn't answer because I knew it would make him worse. I better let him take out his wrath on me. I was shivering but stayed quiet. The wrong move could fuel his anger. I never got to guess which was the right move either...

He got up...I knew what was coming... The unbuckling noises filled the room leaving me breathless.

Wasting no more time. He started to hit my legs.

"I fucking told you to stay there,"

"You ran towards me just to save that fucker you just met,"

"And you aimed me with a gun,"

" I'm your owner who fed you over a year,"

"And there you were defending a stranger,"

" You worthless, whore,"

"Hahaha, scream as much as you want,"

He was beating me mercilessly. But this time was more intense. I couldn't feel my legs anymore.

It was obvious he was out of control as he didn't even bother fetching his favourite leather that wouldn't leave cuts. Now, I could feel the cuts and bruises.

Everything was in pain. My vision started to blurry but it didn't knock me out, it became unbearable.

When he was panting, he walked over to me and shook me, "No, love. You can't faint now. We are nowhere done. Something new is to be taught," my ears were ringing as his evil laughs filled up.

He yanked my hair again exposing my neck. He sucked my neck furiously. I was sure he was making painful hickeys again. He inhaled my hair deeply.

"Fuck! You had already made me calm down," he cursed and continued biting my sensitive skin.

I was no longer screaming. Actually, I couldn't scream anymore. I was thankful that he stopped hitting me with a belt. But I couldn't stop sobbing. He quickly removed the restraint from me and carried me somewhere. I couldn't open my eyes.

Now, I thought I knew what's the purpose of Daniel guy's injection. It was to keep me awake, while this cruel man torture me for his own sick pleasures. I felt something soft underneath me.

He laid me down on a bed. Soon after, he hovered me with kisses. He ripped my dress open and left me in my undergarments. I couldn't even move. My legs were numb.

I tried to struggle underneath him because he was also undoing his pants. I started to panic again. No. Was he planning to...?! No! I tried to push him but he kept straddling me.

His hand went down my private part making me squirm. I sobbed, " Please, no. No, "

" Relax, I just wanna show you something new," he said against my lips.

He was rubbing my private part. I felt so ashamed.

His one hand slipped under my underwear and rubbed along there while one hand was pinning down both of my hands above my head. He never stopped sucking and licking my face.

I felt so violated. He was doing it again... and I doubt he would stop this time.

I felt a weird sensation in my stomach. He kept his torture over my core. Was it pleasure? My stomach was knitting a knot.

But it was gone as his one finger pushed inside me slightly. I cried and he groaned, " So tight," He kept his hand not moving from that place.

"S- stop please," I said against his lips sobbing hard. I hated him. I hated all of these.

He pushed his finger further making me cry out, " Oh, my baby girl," he said breaking the kiss and going to kiss along my neck. He started pushing his finger in and out. No! No!! No!!!

It was burning. " Stop. It hurts. I'm begging you. Please," I pleaded.

He looked me dead in the eyes. Then he pulled out his hand and sucked. Ewww.

" Why aren't you enjoying it?" He said almost questioning himself.

"Mi-Micheal-" I whimpered at the callous grip on my thigh. " p-please..."

" Shut up! " His gazed fixed with my own as I silently plead him with my gaze.

I almost start full-blown breakdown at the cold texture of his shirt. He started rubbing the cloth along my forehead, and wasn't gentle with that behaviour. I didn't dare to look away from him as he silently but impatiently clean my face up.

He locked his gaze back at me and slowly leaned in... daring me to move... I couldn't even if I wanted to.

His lips slowly but roughly intruded my mouth while I gasped for air. He pulled away in just few seconds.

" Sleep now," he murmured, "Or we will continue this unfinished business,"

Luckily he got up from me and walked out of the room after pecking my lips.

Damien. His name was Damien all along.

"He had intentionally been breaking the fierce gem into pieces and had unknowingly been decorating the pieces up into a canvas of his miseries."

Chapter 15

1^{5.}

Fluttering my eyes open, it felt like I hadn't been sleeping at all. This time was completely different with anxious thoughts overwhelming my brain. I didn't sleep at all...

My legs were already bandaged. I looked up at the white ceiling. Micheal was becoming worse. He wouldn't hesitate to break me. That was a bitter truth I dreaded... 'He is unpredictable.' He always had been.

All of the events were more like a ridiculous magic trick that was so unreal yet slap me in the face hard.

The Lizzy lady and her so-called husband Sam, And Micheal's twin Damien. Oh, not to miss was Lizzy called Michael, Damien. They must be siblings?? It was a lot to take in and that started to hurt my head. It was him, everything about him make me wanna go insane.

I heard the door click open. Of course, it was him.

"Hey, baby girl," he mumbled and climbed onto the bed. I closed my eyes wishing somehow he would disappear. I just needed a break...

He joined the bed, pulling and hugging me with light kisses, to which I responded with the firm push against his chest. He... didn't seem to mind, as he simply gathered my wrists in one grip and pulled me sideways against his chest.

"How are you feeling?" His chin moved against my temple as he refused to let me go and continued to hold me in his grip.

"I'm tired," I just wanted him to leave me alone. I was too exhausted to face his bipolar episodes. One wrong move could change him into a blood-thirsty maniac within a second.

"I know, baby girl. I just wanna hold you. Daddy knows you're tired," he mumbled but he never loosen his grip on me. He soothingly patted my hair, kissed my jaw and along the neck as if nothing ever happened.

" I'll take you out if you behave," he mumbled brushing his nose along my cheek.

"Leave me alone," I mumbled. I really needed him to stay away from me, which I knew would never happen...

The soft chuckles escaped from him as he turned me around to face him. His firm hand rested on to my nape and the other to grab my butt. "I will never leave you alone. I will cherish you with my loves and kisses," he trailed wet pecks along my jaw.

This man was driving me insane. I guessed he must be in good mood from his current behaviours.

"I won't go anywhere. I wanna sleep,-" I tried to push his face off me, "Please, leave me-" I squirmed as he wouldn't stop sucking my face. Only God would know how I tired of begging not to be touched...

"Hmmm," he hummed and tilted my chin upward, and sucked on my bottom lip, "No," he grinned.

I scowled but it made him growl. He smacked my ass.

" Don't be so cute as fuck. I won't be able to control myself if you keep doing such a face," he muttered with hooded eyes.

I sighed and turned away from him. But he quickly pulled me again. I struggled with a frown. I just want some peaceful sleep. Damn.

"Say what you want? I'll do you a favour. Anything." He smiled down at me.

I stopped struggling. "Anything?" I asked looking up at him. He ran his hands along with my hair and nodded while rubbing my forearm, silently encouraging me to carry on.

"I wanna see my family," I blurted out risking my luck. I could see his jaw tightening. He inhaled deeply with closed eyes.

I quickly said, "I'm sorry,"

'No. No. I'm not ready for his wrath. I'm stupid. I'm so damn stupid.'

I just wanted to check on them if they were doing fine. Just a glance would soothe my aching heart. But it seemed that was too much to ask for..?

" Fine," he mumbled.

Oh gosh. Did he? Did he just agree? Oh lord. I was in shock for a full minute.

I felt a pang of relief when I openly hugged his frame. My tears started to dampen his white shirt and my vision blurred when I felt his hands rubbing circles on my back.

"Thank you. Thank you, Micheal," I mumbled with gratefulness.

" It is Damien, Damien Martin," he proudly said while rubbing my back.

I pulled away and looked at him, " Why did you lie to me about your name?" I asked curiously.

His eyes twinkled as he cupped my face "I wouldn't let you escape and report me. Not for me, it was for your safety. The moment people knew that you are something to me, they will come after you. I won't let that happen," he said cocking his head to the side.

I looked down confused not knowing what does that even mean.

"But all things are set now," he brought up my hands and brushed his lips onto my knuckles. What's meant by that again?

A maid knocked in and placed the soup tray on the table. I furrowed and scooted away from him. I didn't have an appetite.

"You must eat," he said and I shook my head.

"Then, no going out," he raised a brow. He was messing with my head and he was enjoying it judging from the glint in his eyes.

I grabbed the bowl from him. He would change his mind about letting me see my family, he could. But he grabbed the bowl back towards him and raised a spoonful into his mouth. I never understood his gestures at all. He was always unpredictable.

He raised another spoonful towards me with the same spoon. I hesitantly opened my mouth accepting the warm taste. He fed me until the bowl was emptied. That was where I realized he had been helping me empty the bowl? Such a freak about eating meals up.

I yawned. I felt emotionally and physically drained.

"Come on, doll. It's nap time," he put the bowls away after handing me a water glass. I took a few gulps and lazily nuzzled into the sheets.

He pulled the cover over me hugged me embedding my entire body in his arms. It was a warm feeling that seemed to be a rainbow in this cold world.

I smiled at the thought of seeing my family again. At least. . . . .

"The darkness would have saved the dim light, only if the moments of affection weren't taken as granted..."

Chapter 16

1^{6.}

Michael, of course, Damien... he stood in front of a mirror, fixing his suit and keeping his haunted gaze on me.

Maids were fixing my hair and dress, the accessories he had chosen for me. He would take me out again to let me see my family.

I had no idea...if I could keep my sanity intact...It was about 3 in the afternoon. I felt light-headed and my stomach grumbles strangely. But all I wanted now was to check on my family. I would do anything... even if it meant acting all fine like an obedient...girl.

I was lost in thoughts but I could sense burning stares from Damien, he was staring at me through the mirror. He seemed...amused.

Psychopath. Everything about him confuses me.

I followed the sight of his gaze and found my reflection, confirming he really does have a taste in fashion. I looked quite...decent.

With a nod, he dismissed the maids and held out his hand for me. He dragged me out towards his car and tugged me with a seatbelt securely. He drove down the road while glancing at me from time to time.

I was feeling anxious...And of course, excited... Maybe too excited? I could feel his hand grabbing my thigh and stroking it gently. I wasn't paying attention to him. My mind was a mess with the anxiety eating me up.

Would they be okay? And of course, my little sister, Rita..she was my world. I could feel the hot trails of my tears were streaming down my cheeks again. Just thinking about them was miserable for me.

We were driving for about an hour. Then he stopped at a place. It was a restaurant. He walked into the place leaving me in the car alone.

I wanted to get off the car and ran like crazy but who was I dealing with? Damien would catch me like a rabbit and most importantly he was the only hope to get to see my family again. And I didn't even know where I was right now.

The places were all new to me. I doubted if I would even be in LA. It couldn't be. This place was so void of buildings. And I saw a sign, "Mexico city"

What the heck! Mexico?

I could see Damien walking back towards the car. He was holding a package. He handed me the package and started the engine again.

I opened it and found a burger. The fast food, the real fast food. When was the last time I ate this junk... Instead, the daily meal was set with a diet he chose for me.

The sight of a burger made me teared up. It reminded me of my free life, my freedom.

I was still holding the burger in my hand unable to stop crying. Damien was glancing towards me from time to time but he didn't say anything. He let me cry. About another half hour later, Damien pulled up the car and turned his attention to me.

I shuddered at the cold touch on my face. He stroked my cheek with the back of his hand.

He walked out of the car and gestured me to get out. But what caught my attention was we were in a plane field. What the hell?

I looked around while spinning my head. What was he planning?

"We're going to take a flight," a hint of smirk plastered on his face.

What the heck? No, no. Where the hell I am?

"No, I can't. I'm-" I said while shaking my head in disapproval.

" Baby, I don't want you to be afraid of heights anymore. You will have to use it. Or I can use drugs you if you want," he said sternly.

"No. Don't drug me," I blurted out. I didn't wanna ride a plane though.

"What I'm going to do with you, hmm? You don't wanna choose anything " He said amused. What was so funny?!

I furrowed my brows. I was serious about heights. He continued to walk with me still holding me in bridal style. I buried my face in his shirt as I was tired from two hours of riding the car. I hated myself for it.

It was a private plane. Damn. How this man was filthy rich?! I clutched into his neck again as I heard the engine start. God. I was dead. Would I necessarily have to go through this to see my family once again?

It was worth it!!! Worth. I didn't know what was Damien's plan. And I didn't give a fuck about him. Yes, I would endure this. I would not let him angry about anything. I would behave just to see my family once again.

I was picturing my family to keep myself distracted. I was trying hard but my body started to betray me. My head was spinning around. I clutched more onto Damien. He held me close too. I could hear he was whispering sweets to me. I couldn't pay attention to him.

My heart was starting to beat faster in rage. My breathings were uneven. I started to see black dots again. Damien shook me as I started to feel limp.

Then I could see he cursed and pulled out a syringe from his pocket. I whimpered and struggled. Damn, I hated all of this.

I jumped out of his hold and ran towards the opposite chair. But as soon as I get out of his grip, I realized I was in the air. Oh god. How high was this from the ground? My stomach churned with fear and panic started to wash upon me.

I couldn't breathe anymore. But Damien swiftly held me in place and forced a shot in my neck. I cried out... that was hurt. My vision started to blurry and I blacked out.

"Shhh. Take a rest, baby,"

I opened my eyes from touches on my face that was disturbing my sleep. I found myself in the car. I was sleeping on Damien's arm. He was talking to the phone barking as usual. We were in the backseat of a car. And the sight made me happy. The traffic as I always used to see a year ago. I remembered this place immediately. I was back in LA. I couldn't see the driver though.

Damien was playing with my hair. My stomach hurts again making me whimper. Damien cut the phone and held my face with his palms. As usual, he was observing me with those grey eyes.

" Are you okay? How are you feeling?" He asked while patting my hair.

I wanted to say, ' No. Bastard, take me to my family now. Stop all this drama!!' But I decided against it. "Can you take me to my family now? I wanna see them now," I whispered.

He smiled and leaned in to kiss me softly, " As you wish, baby,"

I was paying attention to the outside through the car windows. Everything was memorable. The car windows were black. Yea, of course, Damien made sure of the outsiders not to see through inside.

It was barely visible to the outside even from inside.

I clutched to the car window but Damien instantly pulled me back to his lap and held me in place. "Just a glance and we'll be back to the hotel. Don't try anything stupid," he mumbled softly.

I gulped and nodded.

After almost felt like forever, my street came into view. I couldn't help but broke down into tears. And there I could barely see my house. The car stopped and Damien handed me the telescope. This bastard!!!

But I should be thankful to him in this situation. Even though I was watching through the telescope, my heart clutched desperately. My mouth hung open with joy at the sight of my mother coming outside and standing at the doorway holding my little sister.

She leaned onto the door and said something to my sister's ear making her squeak in amusement. She was teasing her. But her smile faded slowly.

She sniffled and wiped her tears. My father came into view and held her shoulder. They leaned onto each other.

My family, I wanted to run towards them right away. To be in their arms once again. I tried to keep watching them but my heart unbearably twisted in pain.

Before I could say anything, Damien slowly took the telescope away from me. I broke down into tears. I would do anything to be in their arms once again.

And yet, I looked up to meet Damien's emotionless face. He snatched my freedom and my family away from me.

"Take me there," I said with bitterness in my voice.

"No, " he replied calmly.

"Don't you fucking hear me?! Take me to them," I yelled at him. I couldn't control it anymore. I thought seeing them would make me calm down. But it only made me feel strong.

He took a deep breath with closed eyes, "Let's go back to rest. I understand you're tired," He patted my hair but I jerked away from him.

I glared at him with so much hatred. "I won't go anywhere with you. Take me there!" I said. I couldn't give control of myself anymore. The sight of my mother crying broke my heart.

He sighed and pinched his nose bridge, " Head back to the hotel,"

No. No. I struggled like a wild animal.

"Vivan, that's enough," he growled while gripping my wrists painfully. I did something I had never done. I bit down hard on his hands and headbutted him.

He cried in pain and let go of me. I climbed towards the driver's seat and pulled open the door. The driver couldn't get a hold of me because he was struggling with steering.

I successfully opened the car door and jumped out of the driving car. I was lucky because it was driving at a slow speed.

I grunted in pain and rushed into the streets. As usual, the streets were void of people. I was stupidly hoping to get away from him. A pair of strong arms held me by my nape back painfully. Damien yanked my hair eliciting a painful cry.

"You want the hard way, then let's make it the hard way," he smacked my head with the ground...hard...

"The fate mocked her... in the form of hardship...in the form of sharpening bliss."

Chapter 17

1⁷·

It was freezing. I could make out the dim light. My eyelids felt so heavy and my head hurts like a bitch.

The shuffling sounds were heard and in no time, the ice-like water was splashed on me. I could feel my jaws itching from the impact. Damnit. Why would I have to face such torture every time I woke up???

Daniel was looking down at me.

I glared at him as he stood in front of me with a bucket of water. He held an emotionless face with those shining eyes that was much look alike Damien's.

Whatever, I hate both of these crazy twins... How did I even end up here again!!!???

I was tied to a chair in the basement as usual. Oh god. I was sick of all these things. That few moments of Mom and Dad's sight changed something inside me. I needed to be strong. They needed me. My family needed me.

"I won't fall for you and your brother's sick games. Retarded cowards," I snapped at Daniel as soon as he turned to walk away.

He froze and turned back at me. He was just standing there, staring at me, and knitting his brow. He seemed to be irritated. But it was more like he was...confused.

"What? Confused? You both are nothing but selfish morons," I said looking directly in his grey eyes with venom in my voice.

Daniel walked towards me slowly and as soon as he was near me, he raised a hand near my face. I closed my eyes immediately and waited for the slap but it never came. Instead, he patted his finger along the bridge of my nose.

He was staring right at me. Although he was exactly looked like Damien, I wasn't afraid of him. There was something about this Daniel guy. Then he leaned in closer to my eye level. His breath was fanning on my face. I thought he was about to kiss me...but instead, he unlocked the restraints and said, "I would shut up if I were you," he mumbled.

" You two are nothing but sick freaks who would lock up a woman without her consent. You should be ashamed of yourself, " I said with a glare at him. I didn't know what was inside of me. But I was pretty sure I would be dead by tomorrow because I was about to dig my very own grave. Not later, but soon...

"Well, that's not true," a voice boomed. It was Damien. I could hear footsteps echoing.

"Shhh," Daniel made a face while holding up his finger on my lip in shut-the-fuck-up manner and he left with a last glance.

Damien came into the room, stood by the door, and leaned in onto that. He was shirtless. At that moment I knew, that couldn't be good. I free myself from the chair and ran towards the corner. Damien was watching me like a hawk, catching all of my movements.

" That's not true because you're not even a woman,-" he sent a side smirk, "You're just a little girl,"

"Tiny little girl," he raised his hand gesturing it.

I took short breaths trying to regain my composure. I was panting as Damien took a slow step towards me. He stood up pressing his body against mine. I was sandwiched between him and the wall.

"Tsk tsk tsk, why so quiet? " He said while tapping my lip with his finger. "You wouldn't be this quiet when I visit your lovely family," he mumbled. The vile rose in me so I leaned in and spat his face.

He closed his eyes and wiped them away slowly. His hands went down my throat... and he grabbed it harshly. "It's been a whole fucking year that I'm trying to tame your feisty nature. Am I being so nice to you, huh? Say who do you belong to!!!" He barked.

" I hate you, Damien,-" I squirmed as his grip tightened, "Or Michael. I will never be yours," I slowly said.

" I don't think so, my love," he mumbled and started choking me with a death grip. The grip was tightening with each second. "You are already mine, and I had to keep reminding you this fucking reality every damn time!" I felt his hands trembling.

" You're a-a coward. I- If you threaten m-me using m-my family," I breathed out struggling against him.

He let go of me immediately. I dropped down and sucked in the air greedily. "Smart mouth, huh?" He smirked and got up from me to grab something.

It was a water pump. Oh no.

He backed away slowly...and I pressed myself further in the corner hiding my face.

He started splashing me with the water pipe. The pressure and the coolness were killing me. I couldn't help but curled into the corner as he continued to torture me mercilessly. He would not stop until he was satisfied.

After almost felt like forever, he finally stopped. My jaws were quivering and my whole body was numb. I hugged myself tightly intending to hide and intending to back away from the heat radiating from him towering over me.

"Get up!" He hissed. I could see him undressing from the corner of my eye. "Get the fuck up before I make you," my vision was blurry but I could make out that he was shirtless now.

I tried moving my leg but I couldn't. "I can't,"

I looked up at him and that moment he hoisted me up by my arm and pushed my body against the wall. I had to control myself to not lean into his embrace. It was so tempting.

" Kitty doesn't like water, does she?" He mumbled while sucking my already bruised lips, and closing up the space sandwiching me between the wall and him.

" I promise you that I'll fight you till my last breath," I gritted when he pulled away.

" Who cares? I already got you. You can't do anything about that, can you? My sweet doll," his eyes bored into mine as he held up my chin.

"You may have my body. But not my soul," I bit him back making him stumble back and I slapped him as hard as I could.

Before I could even register what was happening, he yanked my hair and exposed my bare neck to him. He bit down where my neck and shoulder meet. The pain was unbearable. He had never done that before. His canines were digging deep into me as he bit down with his might.

I wasn't sure whether I was screaming or I had already lost my voice.

I was struggling like a wild animal but it only makes it worse because his grip on my waist tightened in a twisting pain. I even tried to pull his hair out. But he didn't even budge.

He finally let me go and I lay there holding my neck in unbearable pain. I could even see the black dots in my vision. My ears buzzed with pain. I heard him cursing loudly as he stormed off the room.

I wanna die...--

"Abuse grows from attitudes and values, not feelings. The roots are ownership, the trunk is an entitlement, and the branches are the control."

Chapter 18

1 8.

It was so cold. Everything was cold. My stomach hurts. I missed my mom. If she was here, she would tug me to the bed and sang me her lullaby till I fell asleep or she would make me something to eat. Maybe she could tell me her stories while keeping me warm in her embrace.

I was still on the floor. I had no idea how many hours had passed. I couldn't even move. It was excruciating how I couldn't get used to the pain. I could feel the blood dripping down my neck. I was scared and all of my strengths vanished at this moment. I felt like giving up.

Maybe Damien was right, I was nothing but a little girl...

I could hear footsteps again. No. No. No. I wished I could have disappeared into thin air and never been reborn.

Now, the person was standing near me. I sobbed hard. I still couldn't believe that was happening to me. I tried to move away but I couldn't even open my eyes. Everything was damn hurt. "M- Mommy h- help," I was hyperventilating.

That person gently held me but his touches were painful for me. "Shhh," he cooed. But that cologne, was that Daniel? Because it was definitely not Damien.

He carried me in bridal style. I was scared but also fuming with anger. It was never the option to choose the safer path because everything about Damien led to my suffering. I squeaked out with closed eyes, " Put me down, you bastard,"

His grip was suddenly tightened on my thigh. " Shhh," he snapped.

I opened my eyes and met with a sharply defined jaw. He got defined features like Damien. Ha, another reason to hate him. I shivered at the contact between him and me as Daniel continued to carry me elsewhere.

He placed me on something soft. A maid came in and changed me into dry clothes, after that she put me into bed. I was more like a ragged doll with broken limbs. I couldn't even feel my legs anymore. It was all sore and cold.

Daniel came in again with a box. He was wearing the spectacles again.

He cleaned the wound at my neck. I couldn't do anything but clutched onto the sheets, hoping it would take away the stinginess in my neck. Then he put on the bandages. He kept a stoic face seemingly unfazed by my hateful glares.

He sat on the bed and prepared the syringe without making a glance at me. Ughh. I hated him. I fucking hate needles more.

So I asked him," I-Is that n-necessary?"

Silence... He was only focusing on his syringe as he tapped it a few times. I was watching his every move. But he never glanced at me. With an approval look on his face, the maid held me in place.

I could only turn the other way. My chest was tightening as I felt the excruciating pain. The shot was done and I was a crying mess. My eyes grew heavy and the last thing on my mind was his taunting eyes that held.....pity?

I woke up with a heavyweight on my waist. No need to investigate who it was. It was Damien. He was hovering over me again. He kept assaulting my face and my body. The room was lack of light. It was already night.

The bandage was digging deep into the wound as he was hovering over me harshly. He kissed me roughly while roaming his filthy hand over my body. I could taste something bitter. Was that alcohol?

"Don't you ever try to run away from me," he mumbled against my already bruised lips. "Do you hear me, baby girl?" he slurred. I stayed silent.

He sighed and got up from me. I heard him slam the bathroom door shut. I cursed under my breath because my stomach aches again. After almost an hour, Damien walked out with a towel. The moonlight was shining upon from the balcony. I didn't want to see him any longer so I pretended to be asleep.

I felt the bed dip and Damien joined the bed with a wet body. His hot finger traced the bandage on my neck slowly making me whimper.

" You brought this upon yourself," he mumbled while caressing my face with the back of his hand.

Was he trying to sound like a joke?! That was fucking obvious he did it on purpose. And he was even blaming me now. But arguing with someone like him wasn't even the option. I guessed we were passed that point, he held the power here.

I stayed silent with closed eyes.

"Hey, show me your beautiful eyes," he said while brushing his nose along my jaw.

Not wanting to fight him I fluttered my eyes open. His grey eyes almost shine in dim light. He leaned in again and kissed my eyebrows.

" That's my girl, " he said and got up to grab a tray on the table. It was the soup again. A lone tear escaped... Why should I have to suffer this shit?

But defying him now wouldn't make any difference. So I ate the soup as he fed me although I was on the verge of throwing up. Fortunately, he stopped at the half bowl and left the room.

Not knowing where he went or what happened later that, I blacked out again.

(The next morning)

Oh god. Why is my stomach so hurt? I needed to use the bathroom now! Damien's hand was over my chest firmly. I felt so irritated that I smacked his head. I just hit him.

He growled and held my wrists pinning down the bed. "What the hell you think you're doing?!" He growled.

"I need to use the bathroom," I snapped. He growled but let go of me.

I was gasping for air as I slowly sat up. The pain felt like thousands of needles jabbing on my stomach. My vision blurred...

I rubbed my eyes to see clearly and when I looked down... I saw my crotch was red. The white undie was now tainted with crimson colour. I felt like my head has grown bigger. Was that blood?????!!!!!!!

I screamed making Damien snap his head at me.

What the hell was that????!!!!

"Unknowingly had been tricked into survival while the monster thrives within her callowness."

Chapter 19

19.

There was blood on the sheets too. I was in shock. What the hell was that????!!!!! My stomach burst from the inside? Was I going to die???

I helplessly looked up at him... and his smirk turned into full-blown laughter. He was laughing???!!!

His face stuck with a genuine smile. Before I could blink, he suddenly pulled me into his embrace gently. He made a phone call and I was too confused about the situation. His hands sneaked around me and his head nuzzled into my chest.

He seemed excited. What??? Maybe he poisoned me last night!!! I shivered at the thought but recovered at the relevance, if so I would have died long ago... But... How the fuCk??

The maids rushed inside. I followed my eyes around as they disappear into the bathroom.

Damien was nibbling all over my face and my stomach was twisting with pure annoyance.

He dismissed the maids and tried to strip me off. I slapped his hand away and his eyes grew darker shades. His eyes focused on me with a glint.

"There's nothing I haven't seen, baby girl," he said while rubbing my stomach gently. That felt good... It made me feel better.

He tried to undress me again. I slapped away his hand again and said," What is happening to me?" I got emotional again I could feel tears running down my cheeks. What's wrong with me?

He sighed and held my hand in his. "Let's clean you up," He mumbled against my knuckles.

I was confused. Why the hell he was acting so nice? I let him strip me off because I felt like a mess and there was blood all over my thighs. He placed me down into the warm bathtub and washed me up. That relaxed me instantly. He carefully wrapped a towel around my head. I looked at him confused. I wanted to wash my hair.

I tried to pry off the towel but Damien's hand was stopping me from doing so.

"No. What are you doing?" He said.

"Can't I have little privacy? I want to wash my hair," I snapped back.

"First, you're not going to wash your hair till next week and second, I'll be with you for today," he poked my nose.

That's insane. What was with this man?! Damn, he was acting all sweet again? That was not something surprising. He wrapped me up and dried me off with a towel. He then placed the white towel on the bed and made me sit on it. That's when I realized I was bleeding from my private part.

The hotel room was quite aesthetic as I took a look around while Damien was busy talking to maids.

And there was a maid, whose name was Betty, I guessed. She was one of the maids, she was also a nurse because at the place where Damien first locked me up. It was her who always cleaned up my wounds. It was been a while since I hadn't seen her as Damien changed the maids almost every day.

"Listen to this ma'am. I'll be back," he said while walking up to me and kissing me on the head. "I love you so much. I'm proud of you, Little lady," he chuckled and gave me one last glance before walking out of the room.

Betty said while holding up some clothes to me." Wear this, my lady,"

I checked the items and hang my mouth in awe. The dress was just fine as usual but there was a diaper-like thing tagged on the underwear.

"Is that... a diaper?" I cocked an eyebrow at her.

"No, but you will need to wear this," she said with a genuine smile.

"Are you fucking kidding me? I'm not wearing this shit," I frowned and threw it across the room.

She handed me another panty with that stuff sticking on it.

"Wear this, my lady, then I will explain to you why are you bleeding like this," she grinned at me.

"Am I going to die, right?" I squeaked out.

"No, you're not going to die. Just wear this, my lady," she said amused.

I sighed and wore comfy clothes. That stuff was poking my core. Everything was comfy except that stuff. Then the lady explained to me that was menstruation that will happen once a month.

Damn. I had to learn this stuff at school. But how this thing was happening to me now? I couldn't even relate..... It was all blur to me... It's like I couldn't make out any of those memories...

She was talking to me more about some kinds of stuff but I could barely hear her. I couldn't focus.I was confused. I was scared. I hated myself that I couldn't get to think about my parents because of the throbbing pain. 'I guessed that was the cramps. Girls around my age wouldn't stop complaining about it but now I was totally siding with them.'

I really hated myself for the first time. I guessed I got so-called depression right now??

Damien walked in again with a tray. I was hungry that I snatched it from him and started eating everything on the plate.

Damien said nothing but smiled. A genuine smile stuck across his face and he kept staring at me with those unknown eyes. His eyes were different now. Not anger, not sadistic, not lust. It was more like.... adoration? He was staring at me as if I was a won ticket while I was busy eating. I handed him the empty tray but he kept staring at me the whole time with his chin in his palms. I could never figure out this man...

He dismissed the maids and walked out with the tray.

The pain in my stomach intensified so I laid down on the bed. I heard Damien's footsteps nearing me again. I didn't bother looking up to him. All I knew was the pain in my stomach and that moment..... Mom. Dad. Rita...

I didn't even realize that I was crying as Damien cooed at me and pulled me under the sheets. He placed a warm bag on the side of my tummy and made my back pressed against his chest.

"Shh, baby. The pain will be gone. Daddy promises you. Take rest," he mumbled softly while kissing my earlobes.

He patted my jawline, my hair, and my butt, mumbling 'All mine,' Then he pressed his hand on my left chest gently touching my heartbeat. "You're mine," he mumbled.

He rubbed my stomach gently, it instantly made me relaxed and sleepy.

The last thing I heard was Damien's voice, " My sweet little obsession,"

"The symphonic he used to describe his feeling was the abstract delicacy between a thin line of hope and denial."

Chapter 20

- -

2 ^{0.}

I woke up in the afternoon with Damien resting his hand over my chest. He too woke up as I stirred under his grasp. Didn't he go to his work???

"How are you feeling, babygirl?" He mumbled with a release of tired breath. It was obvious that he was tired as always. He brushed strands from my forehead followed by a lingering kiss on it.

"I'm fine," I snapped. I had to admit that I liked the way he treated me now. Why couldn't he be normal just like this???

"Hmmm, " he hummed while sucking on my lips. I didn't know but somehow I felt so irritated that he was kissing me whatever the hell he wanted. I furrowed my brows together and pushed his face.

He backed off with a huge smile. "Is my baby feeling irritated? Hm?" He chuckled kissing my nose.

I cursed him mentally and tried to get up. Only ended up having my stomach erupt with nauseous pain suddenly. I whimpered and Damien quickly pulled me back into his embrace and placed another warm bag on the side of my stomach.

The only thing that I had on my mind was food... Chocolate?? I was busy thinking about it that I didn't notice Damien was staring at me with his glossy eyes. His grey eyes were most outstanding for me when he was in good mood.

"So beautiful," he mumbled with a smile showing off his perfect teeth. Damn. Why was he smiling like a mad man? Those were real smiles, unlike sadistic smirks.

I got emotional again as the thought of my family flooded... But what could I do right now? I couldn't even move! Maybe I could ask him later to see them once again as he was in good mood???

Now, I was craving my desserts and snacks.

A maid came in with a tray. Damien handed me the tray making me go 'ew' at the food. Vegetables and water. I furrowed my eyes with a grimaced face at him in a questioning manner.

He chuckled and said, " No chocolate or caffeine, baby girl,"

I tugged into the food and ate silently as I had no choice. After finishing the food, Damien pulled me into his warm embrace again whispering how much he... loved me... It had been done to death, I swear...

The rest of the day he spent time with me in bed making sure I was comfortable.

And the maid, Betty, she came at nights to change that stuff. I was disgusted with myself at the sight of my blood on that stuff. Damien never left the room much to my dismay.

I ended up the next three days with Damien in that hotel room...Eat. Sleep. Cramps...

(Three days later)

Finally, that thing had stopped. Damien was cherishing his time with me with everything I wanted except chocolates.

I leaned in at the railing of the veranda and enjoyed the city view of my hometown. I felt so refreshed. I was so happy just to be here. I couldn't even take a step out of the confined room for the last whole year.

Peace. It was pure peace. Excluding the pain and the clingy bastard, these days had brought me a taste of peacefulness.

I felt a presence behind me. Him...

I felt his hand come resting on my stomach, rubbing it, drawing patterns or whatsoever. The air in my lungs was almost knocked out as he suddenly turned me around and his lips crashed on mine harshly. It only lasted a minute or so before he pulled away with a wide grin.

His hands kneaded my nape, almost having me lean into his warmth. "I love you, doll," with a peck he dragged me by my hand leading me in the direction of the couch. 'He does have a thing for having the identical furniture.' Or maybe it was just one of his plans to taunt my sanity with the feeling of dejà Vu floating around?

I felt a tug on my wrist as he silently indicates to me to sit down on his lap. I did as I was told...'There goes his satisfied grin...' Then he started typing things on his laptop while keeping his hand on my back, rubbing small circles as if to distract me from nodding off. Which was odd, because he never really cared what I wished. It was his excessive attention...

Curiosity got the best of me...

"Can I ask you something?" I asked while looking up at his perfect jawline.

"Hm?" He said casually. Like always, I rarely got the answers from him. He simply ignored me or... punished me for Some questions he couldn't ignore.

" Why are you doing this to me? I mean, why you just can't approach me like a normal person in the first place?" I asked and instantly regretted it. I could feel his body tense up. I mentally cursed myself...

He stopped typing and looked down at me. I felt super uncomfortable... I didn't dare to look anywhere near his face. I fisted my hands...scared I would tick him off.

But to my relief, he chuckled. " I'm not a teenager, baby girl. Daddy doesn't do such childish things," he poked my nose teasingly. "And what do you even mean by...normal?" He mused.

" Umm. Something or without kidnapping?" I asked but whispered the last part. But he heard it.

"You want me to take you out?" He laughed again showing off his teeth. I couldn't help but admired how he looked good with that smile. It was somewhat soothing in my mind compared to witnessing 'that sinister look'.

"Kiss me," his eyes hooded as he whispered sensually.

I knitted my brows and pouted at the change of topic.

"Then I won't take you to see them and we're going back-," he said but I cut him off.

I instantly pulled him and kissed him. I did as he did to me. I sucked and licked his lips. He was frozen for like fifteen seconds. But he instantly dominated the kiss and gripped my breasts, having me huffed like a fish out of water from the pain.

I couldn't miss this chance...he would change his mind.

Damien finally pulled away and rested his forehead against mine. "You know that I love you so much, hm? Daddy loves you so much," he muttered as he tightened his grip.

I decided to play along with him. "Yes, Daddy," I answered.

He growled and pulled me into another harsh kiss. "Say it again, baby," he moaned.

"Daddy," I breathed out.

Finally, he pulled away and walked out of the room but not before saying to me that he would come back to fetch me. He looked tensed...

I lay on the bed and dozed off. I hoped my little plan would work.....

"When push comes to shove, it will never be enough to make it on her own."

Chapter 21

------

2 ¹·

I was on the verge of breakdown as I could see mom wouldn't stop crying. She was leaning on the doorframe, looking out to the sky, and crying softly.

Damien held a tight grip on my waist in a warning manner.

He parked just a few blocks from my house. I had been scratching at the door for about an hour while I pleaded with him to give me at most three hours. I couldn't cry anymore. My mom was sitting there like a few blocks away from me and I was in this fucking soundproof car, yearning for her.

Damien said nothing but he kept his stern posture. He seemed trying to calm himself.

I wasn't paying attention to him either. For another two hours, I sat by the window and looked at Mom as she sat on a chair and was knitting something. She used to knit on the veranda till evening...

I could see she was wearing my necklace. She would pick it in her hand and kissed it every minute while tears streamed down her face. She was missing me as much as I missed her. I was happy about that at least. No... I didn't doubt it.

My hands were currently numb from hitting the car windows all the time. All I could do was now leaning on the window glass and trace patterns.

Damien was focusing on his laptop.

It was almost three hours and ten minutes... Anxiety started to overwhelm me as I knew Damien would drag me back to the hotel. I didn't want to go anywhere near him. I wanted mom and dad.

I sobbed hard at Damien's voice, "Time's up," he said sternly as I whimpered.

Then the engine started, I panicked and pounded onto the windows again hoping mom would hear me.

But it was no use. I cried harder and dragged Damien's suit making him furrow his eyebrows. Anger evidently swirling in his grey eyes. "No, please. I don't want to go with yo-" I sobbed but Damien swiftly held my chin.

"Enough is enough. We're going back," he said slowly with closed eyes.

Why he was so angry? He was in a good mood when he said he would let me see my family again!

"But- But-" I squeaked out.

"No buts," he said sternly and drove off as if my pleas were deaf to him.

I couldn't think straight that I pulled the steering wheel making the car almost hit the tree but Damien was skilled enough to stop the car.

I was scared. I was confused. I didn't know anymore. I just- just- let this chance slip off like this.

The silence fell and the tension in the air could be cut with a knife. Only my sobs could be heard in the car. I peaked at Damien. He was clutching the steering wheel so hard that his knuckles were turning white. I backed off away from him as far as possible and cried my heart out.

"I said enough is enough!! You could have hurt yourself!!!!" He yelled and banged his fist on the steering wheel.

He then suddenly turned at me and shot an angry glare. He was beyond furious... I didn't care about his wrath now... But my trembling lips said otherwise. He slowly leaned in and raised his hand. I sobbed and was ready for the slap looking at his hand that was raised in the air.

I glared back at him with tearful eyes. His chest was heaving as if he ran a marathon. He was staring at me like forever and retracted his hand.

"I'll let this aside," he said while gazing at the road ahead. " If you ever try this again, I won't hesitate to make my men visit your family," He seethed.

I sat back down and sobbed quietly scooting away from him. Damien was focusing on the road only and I didn't dare to make a sound, defeated...

The drive wasn't ending so I ended up taking a nap leaning on the car window.

I woke up to a hand rubbing my cheek. His touch was soft that I didn't even know if this was just a dream. I took a look around that I realized I was still in the car in the middle of a huge field of... Flowers!

He gently led me out of the car and placed me on the car bumper. His hands were on either side of my thighs. "I was upset that you were yearning for your family more than me," he said inhaling my hair.

What???!!! Why did he say as if he was something to me? I wanted to shout, ' Oh yea, I yearned for my own family and I hate you bastard! Go and jump off a cliff and die! '

But I already knew that would be digging my own grave. I didn't want to be killed by furious Damien, at least not now... I have a family who was missing me and waiting for me to come Home.

I said nothing but took a look around. I was in the middle of nowhere but filled with colourful flowers. It was already evening so the breeze and the fragrance were luring me to swing myself into the air.

Damien turned my face at him and kissed me as his life depended on it. "I love you, baby girl," he mumbled.

I said nothing but sighed.

He chuckled... I could never understand which part of this situation was funny...., " I'll be waiting here. You can walk around. Just be in my sight," he pecked my cheeks.

I eagerly stepped out into the flower field and took a deep breath. I took a look at Damien again as he was glancing at me with a phone in his hand.

I was greedily picking up the flowers in my hands. I felt so good. Relief washed over me at the touch of these natural flowers, unlike the beautiful yet creepy flowers that Damien would bring into the room every day.

Then I realized he was trying to shut me out of the real world...

But why was he suddenly good and tried to fulfil my wishes? Did he think I could forgive him for what he did to me in the past? I pressed along the tattoo place where he forcefully and intentionally hurt me. The scars might fade away from my skin but the scars in my heart would never.

Damien was barking at someone on the line. I watched him from distance and pressed my lips into a thin line. "I will hate you no matter what," I mumbled to myself.

That was a promise, Damien Martin.

" The words she had been portraying her situation became the abuse itself, mantling the fragile soul."

Chapter 22

----

(22)

Damien let me stay in the field till sunset. I was exhausted... But it was refreshing to have such fresh air after such a long time. I really didn't remember when was the last time I touched flowers... Because the ones Damien sometimes brought to me were unearthly beautiful and gave off a creepy vibe. I instantly plopped down into the fresh grasses.

I longingly gazed into nothingness. It just didn't make sense till now... How my life changed upside down in the blink of an eye from the past two years to this moment.

I felt him nuzzling into my neck as he held me from behind...my time was up... I just let him lift me by my arms. He drove me back to the hotel but he immediately left after making a rushed call.

Why he was such in rush? Not that I cared... I shrugged off and pulled the cover over me.

About three hours later...

I woke up and jumped out of bed as I heard the loud bang on the hotel door. I quickly hid under the bed not knowing what to do.

I heard voices, the voices that didn't seem to disappear anytime soon as the footsteps loudly approached. I was panicking. It was too real to be an illusion... So that meant I was in danger???

"Where is she?" A voice said. But wait... that voice. Lizzy?! Damien's sister?

The door swiftly opened with a loud bang had I broken down into tears. I didn't dare to make a sound as I slapped my mouth shut. Then, a hand removes the sheet that was covering my spot. I screamed out and backed off while sobbing.

I hated it. There were more than ten people in the room with guns. And the scariest thing was their attention on me. I curled into a ball and hugged my knees. This was too much.

"Guys, you can't just corner her like that...get out," Lizzy fumbled through them.

It helped me a lot. I could breathe properly right now. She turned her attention towards me making my breath hitch.

"I won't hurt you. I promise," she said in a surrendering manner. "You need to come with me, honey," she smiled warmly. I didn't trust her at all.

I clutched my hands in my chest and stared at her catching her movemen ts... searching for the unknown threat.

"Lizz. Get the girl. We need to leave, now" a voice boomed. I started to panic again as she started to approach me. No. No. No. I couldn't breathe again.

She noticed that and stopped her steps. I was struggling to breathe.

"It's okay, honey. Calm down and count to three. You got it?" I heard her voice again.

Lack of air was striking me real hard which made my lungs desperately puff for oxygen. I dropped down onto the floor and shortly after that a sharp pain passed through my neck and everything went black.

(Start of Flashback)

Summer. Summer. Summer. I had been waiting for this after the exhausting last day of school. It just never seemed to end the circle of students getting excited for the first day of a school year and the very last day. Socialising came so naturally that I didn't bother locking myself up in the boring room, so I was going to have some fun. Hanging out with friends!

We gathered at the bus stop. Seeing a gorgeous boy coming along with my friends had me frown at the familiar face.

Then it had hit me and clutched my hands over my mouth. Was it Henry? The one who was with me as a bestie when we were only in Grade-1?!! I felt myself heating up as I clutched my hands over my forehead. I was surprised to see him again after a long time... He was surprised to see me as well as they approached, but not a word was said between us that seemingly hurt my feelings a bit.

Maybe he was shy...

But I couldn't help but catch him staring at me from time to time.

I shook my thoughts and fidgeted my fingers. How could someone like him possibly interest me? Maybe he was just trying to process things... He was glowed up with that look though... as he had always been.

We were having fun and laughing like mad kids in the cafe as the stoner in our group was a comedy to us.

I walked along with my friends in the streets while giggling and saying gibberish. I could feel some weird sensation in my stomach as if I was being watched. That feeling was there since in the cafe.

So I told my bestie that I had a weird feeling. She said nothing but made a face and then asked Henry if he could walk me home had my jaw dropped down.

I was blurting nonsenses. I felt like I could die by hitting my head against a tree.

I tried to say 'no' but Henry's insistent had my stomach flipped. Then he walked me home. As we passed the alley. A nudge to my hand warmed my intire face until I felt an arm clutch my waist gently. I was surprised and yet excited. My head was hot as hell and the back of my ears were itching, as Henry rested his forehead against mine breathing deeply and him clutching my nape tightly. As Henry was about to kiss me, I could feel he was ripped apart from me.

And there a man was shouting and punching him as if he was ready to kill Henry. I was frozen in my place as I watched the bloody scene folding in front of me. I screamed unintentionally, but that made the mystery man turn his head at me leaving me breathless.

The unforgiving grey eyes that seemed like a beast staring into my soul, readying to pounce upon me. The scrupulously flawless face failed to hide the gruelling cruelty lingering over his spine chilling aura.

I tried to get back on my heels and ran. But the man roughly shoved me into his hard chest as I felt him nuzzling into my neck from behind. He then quickly turned me around and shoved me into a nearby wall, making me cry out in pain.

I was about to scream for help when he forcefully sucked my lips. This couldn't be the way it was supposed to be!! I tried to struggle but he didn't even budge. He swallowed my muffles and continued to claim my lips hungrily.

An idea popped out of my head and I crouched down his private part making him back off from me. I ran as fast as I can. My ears were ringing as the survival instincts kicked me when my legs felt like jello by a growl sounded from a stormed- like- grey-eyed stranger.

A pair of strong arms yanked my hair making me cry out in pain and fear. I felt my face muscles throbbing as the anger and frustration rose. I managed to face that grey-eyed bastard and I slapped him ...hard... I didn't know how he would feel but my hand was on pure hell as the stinginess lingered.

His face was turned to the other side. I could see his face was getting red and his veins popped out. And other things I knew was an unbearable sting on my cheek and I passed out. That guy had slapped me...

Hard...---------

"He had been refusing about fully gotten to know his own hidden recesses, blind alleys, well shafts, dark barricaded doors, and chased after a mere reminiscent of his trauma RECKLESSLY."

Chapter 23

23)Hurt. Everything was hurting. I found it difficult for me just to open my eyes. But soon as I could, I found myself in a red Room. Almost everything was red, including the sheets that were laying heap on my body.

Sitting up slowly, I checked myself as if a limb was missing. Then the realization hit me, Henry tried to kiss me, and- and- a mystery man beat him up.

'Click' my thoughts were interrupted by the sound of the opening door. The opening door was followed by a man, he was the one who beat Henry, and h- he- also slapped me.

My breath hitched as those grey eyes settled upon me.

"I see you're awake," his voice crept chills all the way down my spine.

My throat dried up taking in his neat appearance. There's no way this Adonis had to be someone I know, someone with... A Gun. A gun!?

For the first time, I was scared for my life. He started walking toward me and I backed up towards the bedpost while tugging my hands in front of me in a protective way. He slowly sat down on the bed and touched my foot that was under the cover. I quickly yanked it off making him growl.

He continued to touch and grab my feet gently with one hand. I yanked his hands off and brought my knees to my chest. All I knew was fear. And yet his handsome face wasn't helping me at all. He sighed and looked down at my feet, put down the gun on the other end of the bed, and gently approached and pulled my feet in his hand placing them on his lap.

I just stared at him... puzzled.

"Listen, I know you might have many questions," He said while rubbing my toes with his thumb. "I'll answer all of your questions once you calm down," The calmness in his voice had almost soothed me.

I didn't dare to speak because I knew my smart mouth well. I didn't want to die... yet...

"Call me Michael. Okay?" he smiled at me.

I was lost in thoughts. What I was doing here? If he kidnapped me, what was his real purpose? My parents weren't that rich to trade me with money. Damn, was I going to die?

"Vivan?" Alarms went off upon hearing him mumble my name. What the heck?! How did he know my name?! I furrowed my eyes and I felt the rage inside me. Damn, Vivan. Focus!

"What I'm doing here?" I snapped at him.

"I'm keeping you. You will be staying with me," he added, "Here," The calmness in his tone and the determination set in his glazing eyes terrified me to the core.

"An-and why is that? I don't even know you!" I snapped angrily.

"You can get to know me, later. We have plenty of time," he said amused this time.

"Listen, Mister, I don't know who the hell you are or what I'm doing here. So, I'm leaving," I said and tried to get up but his hands were holding my feet tightly.

His chest was heaving up and down as if he was trying to calm himself. Then he suddenly climbed on top of me making me scream and hit him.

"Shhh. Shh. Calm down," he said while pinning my hands down on the bed. I noticed he was trying to be gentle with me but no. His weight was crushing my body.

He patted my hair and smiled while gripping both of my hands in his hand. I felt the back of my eyes burn.

"Let me go. I wanna go home!!!" I screamed.

"But you're home now, baby girl," he smirked.

"Don't call me names you freaking sick bastard," I seethed and tried to wiggle out from him.

I could see his eyes darkening, "What did you just call me?" He suddenly gripped my chin in a painful way that I gasped out for help.

I knew I was fucked up. How could I be so stupid? Damn, Vivan, cooperate if you wanna live. I didn't know what to say so I kept quiet swallowing my sobs. His grip on my chin was loosened up slowly.

"Shhhh. I'll let this aside because it was your first time. Okay, baby girl?" He said while rubbing his thumb under my chin. What a psychotic bipolar asshole!!!

"Please, just let me go home, I swear I won't tell anyone about this," I sobbed desperately, scared of what would he do to hurt me again.

His eyes glazed over me and blankly stared at me as if he couldn't hear my pleas.

"So beautiful," he said while tapping his finger on my lips. He leaned in and sucked on my lips forcefully again. He kept on hungrily sucking and licking my lips while tugging my wrists down the mattress with one hand.

He ran his hands through my hair while sucking the life out of me. I couldn't breathe as his face was tucking on my face completely. I mumbled pleas that I couldn't breathe properly.

As almost I could die, he pulled away with a wide grin on his face, and let go of my hands. I sucked in a breath and coughed as my lungs were on fire. I just wanted to wipe that face off him.

I was beyond angry. How dare he was?!!!! I slapped him again. "Go to hell, you bastard!!"

He swiftly grabbed my neck in his hand tight in a warning manner. "Watch your mouth," he said slowly.

I was scared that his grip was tightening as seconds passed. "What do you want from me? " I snapped at him.

"That's an interesting question," he said with a smirk. He slowly let go of my neck.

I felt all the heat rushing up to my forehead as I saw him grabbing his gun and hovering over me again. He rubbed the gun along my jawline making me whimper in fear. "You will find out soon, my love," He mumbled looking down at my lips while licking his lips.

"I swear my parents don't have much money. You wouldn't get much money for my sake, please. I wouldn't tell anyone.. please," I tried to reason with him but my lungs seem giving up.

His eyes darkened and he got off me. He sat down next to me and pulled my legs to him again. He kissed my feet and said while looking at me with those scary yet beautiful grey eyes, " You're mine," then he stood up leaving me in that room locked.....

---------------------------------"The insensate one would never miss a trail of consolation for their deeds. As if... nature trained them to be..."

Chapter 24

----

(24)

I was trying to open the locked door desperately.

About half an hour later, I was still rushing around the room like a rat, hoping I would find something useful or an escape route. My legs protested but anxiety continued spurring me with anticipation.

The noises against the floor seized my movements. I quickly grabbed the lamp and flat myself against the wall, next to the door. A person came in and I used all of my strengths to hit that person in the head. That person's loud growl resonated as I tried to rush out. As almost I barely could make a step, that person grabbed my ankle making me stumble forward.

My eyes burned with tears while I snapped my head back at him...Furious Michael holding his bleeding head. He was groaning with a tight grip on my feet. I didn't think twice before kicking him in the face making him lose the grip on my ankle.

I sprinted down the hallway and found myself in nothing other than a maze-like route. There was a hell hole of rooms. Where the hell would I go now?!

As almost I could get in a room, a vice grip yanked my hair knocking the air out of me. It was him, Michael. With a gruelling grip on my stomach, he dragged me, as if I was a sack of potatoes.

I couldn't do anything because the pain was unbearable and struggling made my head hurt more as if he was trying to pull my brains out of the skull. I could see his blood was dripping down his jaw, and the veins were popping out, ready to kill me? My heart was in my throat and my stomach sank in fear.

He gripped my shoulders and pulled me uptight just to look me dead in the eyes, without blinking, he roughly pushed me to stumble over the lamp I used earlier. His face lack of any emotions as he towered over me and banged my head against the bedpost... repeatedly.

I woke up to a hand rubbing my cheek. I met with familiar grey eyes. My breath hitched and the back of my eyes burned, the unleashed frustration washed out as hot tears.

I kept staring back at him as he tilted his head in a bone-chilling manner. He raised his hand to my face making me flinch and whimper.

But...he only wiped my tears.

"Rule No.1 Don't try to escape," he stated lowly as if he was trying to make sure I heard it right.

"Rule No.2 Don't disrespect me," he stated calmly.

I looked back at him in disbelief. My brows furrowing. What? Seriously?!

I gasped at the weird texture of his hand as he grabbed my nape. "Rule No.3 Don't resist me and my touch," he mumbled while licking his lips. He can't be serious.

I leaned near his face and spat. He swiftly yanked my hair making my neck exposed to him. He sucked on my skin furiously making me twist like a wild animal. His hot breath hit my sensitive skin as he slowly retreated.

"Don't disrespect me," he said while pulling away.

I just closed my eyes and cried not knowing why this was happening.

"Whatever you do, there will be consequences. But I'll give you time to adjust. But I won't tolerate it next time. It means I'll punish you. In ways, you can't imagine. Okay, baby doll?" He said and sucked my lips softly... unexpectedly.

"W-Why me?" I seethed.

"You're meant to be mine," he mumbled and kissed me harshly again.

"You're a freaking psycho," I sobbed.

He pulled away with a sadistic glint in his eyes. "No, baby. I'm yours," he smirked.

"Go to hell, you freaking pedophile-" I said but was cut off as Michael grabbed my chin with a death grip. Fury laced his eyes.

"Don't call me names," he seethed.

"You're hurting me," I cried out as his nails were digging into my skin.

He let go instantly and stared at me blankly. "I might hesitate to hurt your pretty face sometimes. But your beloved ones meant nothing to me," he shrugged.

"I swear I'll kill you by myself if you dare to touch them, you Basta-" I was cut off by a harsh slap across my face. I thought my jaw was broken. Tears were uncontrollably rolling down my cheeks.

"I hate you," I mumbled.

He seemed to get caught off guards and yanked my hair again."What did you just say???!!!" He growled.

"I said, I hate you, moron!" I angrily spat.

He slapped me hard again on the same side. I cried out at the burning assault.

My heart rate accelerated looking up at his fury filled demeanour. He quickly release the restraints, yanked me out of the chair and threw me hard across the floor. I backed away weakly. He crouched down to my level and whispered, "Are you asking for punishment?"

I furiously shook my head 'no' scared of what he would do to me.

But the next second, he just laughed and laughed. I just stared at him, unable to move my frozen body. He looked like an entirely different person."I won't take 'no' as an answer. You're misbehaving...my LOVE," he spat as if the words were venomous. Then he started carrying me over his shoulder walking up to somewhere.

I hit his back and pulled his hair but he didn't even flinch. I was screaming my heart out to the point of gagging.

Once I realized that he was taking me back to that room, I squirmed and bit down his ear.

With a loud gasp he dropped me down onto the floor and I lay on my bum. I tried to get up and ran towards the door but he swiftly pounced on me and threw me onto the bed roughly.

He climbed on top of me and pulled out handcuffs from the drawer. I screamed at the top of my lungs. He easily handcuffed me and rolled me back exposing my butt on his lap.

"Don't you dare make a sound!" He growled ferociously. At that momen t...I knew I had pushed the limits.

I cried out at the lingering sting on my bottom. He .. was spanking me??!

A hand came in front of my face and the tape texture was plastered, sewing my lips shut. I started to panic as my screams were muffled, completely at his mercy.

He was spanking me mercilessly.

I lost count and laid there helplessly.

My heart was clutching painfully.

He turned my face to his side as I was burying my head in the sheets. He roughly pulled the tape off me and had me yelping and whimpering.

" Say 'I belong to you'" he growled.

I kept quiet making him furiously turn me back to face him, tie my wrists to the bedpost and hover me while crushing me with his inhumane weight.

I closed my eyes and sobbed.

His grip became unbearable with him shouting at my face, "Say now or I'll do something I would regret!"

I squirmed under him helplessly. This man was sick. All of this is wrong. ..so wrong...

He roughly ripped my thin gown apart. My chest exposed to him. An alarm went off in my head. No. No. No!!!!

I screamed again as he harshly sucked the skin just above my breasts. "I- I belong t-to you," I cried out hysterically.

He instantly brought his face back to me and the stinging pain followed with an assault on my jaw. He drew blood off the bite on it. "Don't ever forget that you are mine."

(End of Flashback)

"He had hoped to walk away with the stolen frosting heart, while she had been chasing the maple leaf."

Chapter 25

----

(25)

I woke up, disoriented not because I had just forgotten what happened, the anxiety crawled up and shivered my nerves as my fingers flexed to feel the soft mattress under me. Yes, my limb is still intact.

My head was spinning around.

What exactly happened? Mom. Dad. Damien. Flowers.

And intruders! Lizzy? I did remember she gave me a shot in the neck. The thought of that had my throat dry.

Wait... for what? Was I being kidnapped again? What the hell was going on?

I gulped and stared at the door as I heard footsteps and hushed whispers. The blonde guy, Sam, and Lizzy walked inside with welcoming smiles...way too much.

They were walking gently as if their steps could break me. Maybe they can..., I didn't like them staring at me.

I clutched the sheets and observed their every movement. Sam sat on the couch in the corner. Lizzy was still standing with her folded hands.

"Hey, umm. Are you hungry? What do you want to eat, sweety?" She asked making me realize that my stomach was empty.

I stared back at her confused. What the hell was going on and all this behaviour?

"Why am I here? " I mumbled.

I heard Sam sigh. "We saved you from Damien, not exactly like that but we can hide you from him, " he sighed, "for a certain period," Sam said with his gaze elsewhere.

Hide me? From him? But, my family? Oh my god. My family!!! Damien was going to kill them. No.

I started to panic at the thought of Damien hurting them because of me. Damien was truly a lunatic. He wouldn't hesitate to hurt them. Now, this would only add up to his many reasons to finally orphan me...

The unbearable pain ripped through my lungs and I couldn't breathe. I sewed my eyes shut tight as the ache in my chest grew unbearably. The nerves and muscles became almost like icy thorns that spike me from the inside.

"Hey, sweety. Are you okay? Breathe. Just breathe. Sam, do something," I heard Lizzy's panicked voice.

"M- My parents," I squeaked out while fisting my hands and crying. There were just stars and dots in my vision. I just couldn't breathe.

"What's happening?" a harsh voice rasped.

As almost I would blackout, I felt an arm and soft lips on me. Later then, that person started filling my lungs with air making me snatch back into the lights.

I felt something wrapped around my eyes. That person was holding the back of my neck and straightening my throat. I couldn't move. I didn't know what that person was doing but I instantly was breathing again.

I was freaking out at my thoughts. Damien was a man of his words. I couldn't imagine how would he be furious right now. He would take his rage out on my family...he said he would...

Why did they bring me here? What did they want from me? What was the reason? What if my parent's life was in danger because of them? I sobbed hard with my intruding thoughts and excruciating feeling of helplessness.

"Breathe. Slowly," a soothing voice said.

That voice was striking me like a lightning strike. Strong, intimidating but so gentle. I did as the voice told me.

" What's your name?" The voice cooed.

"Vivan," I unconsciously answered.

"Okay, Vivan. I promise I won't hurt you. Do you believe me?" The voice said again and I felt the cloth over my eyes be removed.

I met with light green eyes that were staring down at me. His nose was almost as sharp as a point. Couldn't deny he was....a handsome man.

I felt the back of my eyes burn as I kept staring and I started to panic again.

"I've promised. I won't hurt you, Vivan," he cooed.

Somehow, I could regain my breath as he was holding my neck in such a professional way."Trust me, " he cooed again.

Before I could say anything else, I heard a loud gunshot go off. "Seems like we got companies,"

He then looked down at me. Then I felt pressure on my neck.

"By the way, I'm Mateo. Mateo Devin," I heard that green-eyed man said before everything went black again.-----------

"She was just resting. But she longed for the end of agony."

Chapter 26

(26)

Mom?

The image of a woman that seemingly did not leave my head had pinned me to the state of a statue. A woman who looked just like her from behind stood firmly a few steps away from me. I was in a very very dark place.

"Mom?" I called out.

She turned around. Her hands were tied with a handcuff and her tears were blood. She was quivering.

"Look what you did," she mumbled and motioned her head at a weird angle.

Dad and my little sister were laying lifeless. They looked so pale. I rushed over to them and observed that they both got shots in their hearts. Bullet wounds.

I snapped back my head at my mom as I heard a gunshot go again. The image of her collapsed and I saw Damien was holding the gun.

I screamed at the top of my lungs as my whole world was collapsing. My family. I was supposed to protect them. It was because of me.

It was because of me...____

____

The headache now I was feeling was just like being hit by a brick. Damn. Why was I always had to wake up with a terrible pain somewhere on my body every damn time? 'Was it my fault? He wouldn't hurt me if I obeyed him.'

I shot up awake and took a look around me. What? It looked like I was in a motorhome.

I shuffled around a bit and checked the place. Everything here was clean and neat. I mentally noted that I have to go back to Damien before he went crazy and most likely trying to keep his oath to 'make-me-regret'. I hoped to never get on that side of him.

My bare feet touched the dry grass as I stepped down through the open window. As almost I tried to step my fourth step, a voice rumbled out of nowhere " I thought you trusted me,"

I snapped back at him and narrowed my eyes at his figure sitting few feets away from me. How did I not notice him??? It was the guy who saved me, Mateo Devin. But his stare made me feel uneasy...a lot.

"Going somewhere?" he said with folded hands.

"What about my parents? Are you saying that I should hide somewhere else after putting them into the mouth of the beast?!" I snapped angrily.

"I did try to save your parents. But Damien is no fool either. He had secretly set up plans to keep your parents in his grasp." he said calmly as if it was a sort of business.

"I'm not sitting here and letting that bastard torture, my parents, for my sake," I seethed.

"So what? Are you planning on hitting him and begging him to let your parents go?" He mocked.

"I. Didn't. Ask. Any. Of. You. To. Save. Me. Or. Anything. Like. That!" I snapped back angrily."Do you think I stayed stuck with him for over a year for no fucking reason?! He will fucking kill them!!!" I cried as I couldn't control it anymore.

I could imagine how Damien was holding a gun ready to take someone's life without hesitation. I already saw what he did to one of his gang.

"He won't kill them if he still wants you. Don't worry," he stated.

"Don't worry?! Don't worry!? You..." I pointed my finger at him," better shut your mouth and let me call to him," I yelled.

At the thought of calling him, I thought about the phone. Yes, somewhere on this truck will have a phone. I tried to walk past and get on the truck but that Mateo guy walked up and crossed his arm over the door sealing the entrance.

"He can track you, Vivan," he said while furrowing his face.

"You know what? I don't give a shit," I tried to push his hand away but I couldn't touch him.I was scared to touch him. It felt so wrong... That sense of loyalty suffocated me until I further backed...I don't understand why it felt wrong to touch anything...I closed my eyes and let the endless tears fall again.

I hated myself more for being such pathetic.Damien ruined me in just one fucking year.

I raised my hands to push his hand again but I was frozen. My muscles were tensed.

"Vivan, Calm down-" he started.

"Please, let me call and convince him not to kill my family. I- I- don't even know they're still alive or not," I sobbed into my palms.

"I won't let that happen. It was not only about you. But for everyone's safety. Damien was nothing but a lunatic." he sighed. "But don't worry. I will kill him myself," his voice monotone.

I was confused. Did he want to kill Damien? Then what I was doing here?

"Why did you bring me here? " I said.

"I'll keep you safe here, and I will try my best to locate your parents. In order to keep low, we must avoid anything that will give away our location. Is that clear?" he stated.

Safe? I didn't understand that word. I felt that anxiety eating me alive. Safety wasn't the term I had grown out over the years. I didn't feel anything but that false sense of assurance by being on Damien's good side, the assurance he wouldn't hurt me at that moment, the assurance that would vanish the moment I did something disapproving.

This Mateo got to be kidding me. I leaned near him and crouched his part making him groan and fell holding onto that. I rushed inside the truck and locked the door before he could get inside.

I was shaking like a leaf as I tried to find a phone. Finally, I found and started typing the number as I heartily remembered Damien's number. But my shaky hands were not helping me at all. The thought of him torturing my parents had me tears springing.

"Hey, hey, put the damn phone down. I will tell you why you're here," I heard Mateo guy yelling and pounding on the door.

My hands were shaking and I was typing the wrong numbers. Finally, I typed the right one and was about to call when the phone was snatched from me.

Mateo had opened the door with an extra key and dragged me out. I struggled against his grip and screamed my head off. I was blindly frailing kicks. I felt that suffocation of the vile unwanted touch on my body. I wanted to give up, just take it, and let anything happen, but I couldn't stop that nauseating chills of loyalty towards...HIM?

I couldn't make sense why would it feel so tormenting yet, so relieving?

When I calmed myself down, I was already seated on a chair and Mateo's back was facing me.

"You looked so much like her. And I can't watch you being tortured by that fucker. I won't let such a thing happen to you again," He mumbled.

"Again? Her? Who? What the hell are you talking about?" I said.

He sighed and looked at me sideways rather annoyed. I kept on staring at his side face until he sighed deeply and started speaking.

"My little sister, Gabrielle..." The silence fell upon and I shifted uncomfortably.

"She was a really sweet girl. " He sighed. "You have her features." He said while observing my face.

" She was just a young girl who believe, trust and fall in love so quickly. She didn't know any better. She became friends with that fucker and soon into a relationship. I tried to keep her away from that fucker as he started acting over-possessive," his voice started to come out as a mumble.

"I tried... I tried everything I could. But you know. Martin's family was filthy rich, we were nothing compared to them. And she was being tortured by that fucking sadist. I couldn't afford anything about that. I was barely nineteen," he sighed. I was listening to him carefully.

"And he- he did force her to marry him at that very young age and took her somewhere else," he was now sniffing.

"When I saw her again at the hospital she was dying. She said as her last words holding my hand in her little hands, 'Don't sacrifice your life for revenge,' "

I could see his tears... trailing...never ending.

" And that fucker didn't even let me see her when she died," he wiped off his tears. " I waited for ten years. I was preparing. I won't let Gabrielle's words fade," he sighed,

" My sister, Gabrielle had Xenophobia. Pretty much what was happening to you right now. But her phobia was born with her. And that fucker used that against her not to leave him, " He mumbled.

I started to realize why Damien locked me inside a room for over a year. He was trying to mould me like that Gabrielle girl. So he tortured me and did all those things because I reminded Gabrielle off????!!!!

Unbelievable!!!

"But what about my parents?" I shattered.

" Trust me. He won't kill them because he wants you. And he believes you will love him back," Mateo stated.

Love?

"For some reason, at that moment, the warranting pity overwhelmed the realisation... too inebriated to see past her own callowness."

Chapter 27

----

(27)

    I was currently laying on my stomach with a book in the trunk. It had been a week. No sign of Danger. Of course, the lump in my throat never goes away as I shivered with the slightest noise.

That was suffocating but Sam and Lizzy came along and spent time with me.

I looked out of the window only to find Sam sitting near a log with a cup in his hands.I wished I could relax and enjoy the serene silence since we had parked somewhere in a forest. Who am I kidding?? I couldn't even stand straight for 10 minutes as lack of sleep kicked in.

Overthinking had me agitated throughout the night...

I hadn't seen Mateo since the day he told me about his terrible past. It was more like a surprise for me. A surprise that aggravated my anxiety...

The thought of Damien doing such a thing made me disgust and hate him with all of my guts more and more. Damien was not in terms of humanity. The lack of empathy is shown in his glazing eyes.

I even wondered how could he bear my ass without killing me on the spot whenever I provoked him.

My thoughts were interrupted by a tap over my shoulder. It was ....Lizzy...

'I had no choice but had to bear their touches.I had found out I should fight him back by not allowing him to take over my own sanity. Even if it wouldn't do anything to his doings, it would help me not to collapse.'

'The Isolation. That was what he wanted. He wanted to snatch and lock me up from the world.'

I wrapped myself with a blanket and followed her outside. She gestured for me to sit down on a log as she handed me a mug. It smelled.. chocolate...

The whole week, Lizzy tried to make a conversation with me, but I didn't want to talk about anything... My mind was blank.

Sam guy, didn't talk to me instead he looked at me without sympathy whatsoever.

I learned that Mateo was planning on using me to trap Damien. And thus why he went off, planning something for the whole week. I felt uneasy as nauseous churned in my stomach. I didn't know what Mateo was capable of, but what I know was, that if something went wrong, it will be Our Doom.

I was thinking if Mateo wanted to kill Damien then what was Mateo doing with Lizzy? Lizzy was Damien's sister after all. Does she know anything about Mateo's sister??

I shook off my thoughts. "None of my business" I mentally noted.

" Vivan..." Lizzy let out a whisper, "Wanna try some soup? You haven't been eating well," I heard her mumbling as I looked down at my hot chocolate mug. I wasn't planning to talk to her or anyone else. I was worried sick for my parents...

With an exasperated sigh, she stood in front of me so closely making me a bit uncomfortable.

She sat down at eye level with me as I kept avoiding her gaze. I flinched as she touched and pulled my hands into her warm hands.

The touch was ...amazing. Warm.

Her hands were unlike Damien's cold hands those were ready to break if I made one wrong mistake.

'No matter how small the mistake was, Damien had always made me suffer in the worst ways.'

The touch in Lizzy's gentleness feels like securing me. The assurance.

"Want me to tell you how are you feeling, honey?" She smiled while patting my hands on her hands soothingly.

I couldn't help myself anymore. I was scared of everything. Scared of being tortured, hurt, and threatened by my parents' lives. "I'm scared," I sobbed and she reluctantly wiped my tears off.

"I'm so sorry that I came to know that late, sweety," she said while rubbing my hair. "I won't force you to tell about what happened. But you have to understand that there's a life ahead of you," she mumbled.

I didn't say anything I just sobbed.

"Honey, look at me. It's not your fault," Her words struck me as I meet her teary gaze. "Whatever he said about his actions will not justify and so his mental health. He had done this before... And I won't let it happen again,"

I cried. I just cried. I never felt helpless this much before, and somehow my heartache at the mention of him, I wished he would try and soothe me with his malicious lies that I didn't have to worry about anything. That false sense of security had wrapped me up to the point I couldn't spend a day without his touch.

"Oh, honey. You're safe now. Don't worry," she said while wiping my endless tears. Worrying would be the first and last thing I would be doing with him ruling my entire existence.

She made me a sandwich. I have lost my appetite but I had to stay strong at least for my parents. I hoped my parents would be able to cure this disgraceful moral of mine. I hoped I get to make it back home. I wouldn't let them leave my sight and I would never leave their sight again.

"What about Daniel? " I asked casually but it took both Sam and Lizzy's attention.

They looked at me and mouthed at the same time, " What??"

I furrowed my eyes at them and observed as if they were lying to me about not knowing who was Daniel. At least, Lizzy must know if she was Damien's sister.

"Damien's twin brother? " I said.

"Vivan, what are you saying? Yea, Damien had a twin brother but he died a long time ago," Lizzy mouthed. And Sam seemed to be in deep thoughts.

Now, I was confused.

"Maybe he didn't die," Sam mumbled and looked at me then Lizzy. "I was wondering how can Damien held captive Vivan for a long time with hell whole of mafia things. Now, the answers are clear. Damien was using Daniel as his copy to show off," Sam seethed again.

Lizzy held her temples and dropped down herself to the ground. Sam was quick to help her up. "Danny, Danny. Then, my Danny is still alive, " Lizzy said with tears in her eyes.

I was about to ask her when Mateo would come back when I heard a car being pulled back.

I got up and rushed towards the car. Sam and Lizzy followed behind me. Mateo got out of the car with a frown on his face making me panic. He must bring good news about my parents! "Are they okay?" I asked him as he leaned his back on the car.

Mateo and Sam were looking at each other as if they were mind linking. Mateo nodded at Sam and Sam walked away.

As Mateo tried to pass me I tried shoving him back although he didn't budge. Touching him felt like touching the larva. "Are you going to tell me what the hell was going on?" I snapped at him although I was trembling like a leaf.

Mateo said to Lizzy, "keep an eye on her," Lizzy nodded and gave me a reassuring smile.

Mateo didn't say anything to me and walked past me. Never looking back and leaving me with Lizzy, confused._________________________________

The next morning,.....

I was in the car trying my luck as I kept changing the radio lines as I wanted to listen to the news. I also shut the doors locked... I just feel the need to do it.

I was changing from line to line the whole time. Until, I heard a reporter say about the body of a man who was around 50s, which was deposed near a lake with two gunshots on the heart.

That was Damien's unique way of killing his victims. I was silently praying as the scene replayed in my mind.

My body was shaking and my teeth were chattering. I quickly turned off the radio and turned the TV on. There, a reporter was standing near a lake explaining how the body was deposed and unrecognizable.

And there behind the reporter, I saw couples of people with suits blocking the view of the body.

The sight of a sweater piece made my whole world feel. Everything was spinning around me. Was it? Was it Dad's sweater? I screamed out so loud as I could see the view of the sweater, the only sweater I knitted for him the first time. Was it him? No!!!!!!!!

"No!!!!!! Dad!!!!!!!" I screamed out so loud that I felt my lungs give up. My whole world was collapsing. What if my thoughts were right? And thus why did Mateo ignore me yesterday???? I bit down my hands so hard and cried out.

And what caught my sight was the phone on the bumper. I didn't think twice about snatching the phone in my hands and typing away the number to that evil.

The call was starting to proceed and I heard a loud bang at the car door. Mateo was shouting and banging with his fists. He was saying something but I couldn't hear him out as my brain was blank and I could only focus on the phone.

I turned my back at the door and put the speaker on as I had decided on no turn back.

"Hello, my love, " I heard Damien's deep voice from the phone out loud clearly.

Within a second, Mateo came behind me and snatched the phone away throwing it across the car. The phone was banged with the car wall and shattered into pieces.

The next words furious-Mateo said was,"We need to leave, now!!!"

---The self-proclaim righteous intelligence about survival would do zero to the one who hadn't even had a life yet.

Chapter 28

("We need to leave, Now!!!" Mateo shouted bringing me back to reality.

My head was more like a bulk of the fire... blazing... burning away my sense along with my brains... Everything was spinning around.I broke down onto the floor and sobbed. This couldn't be real.

Mateo was practically rushing around to clean the area. I was sitting in the backseat in a blank state.

I could see Mateo and Sam were in serious conversation while Lizzy was packing her belongings. Their attention wasn't on me.

I got out of the car and looked back at them.

What if Dad was dead? If so, then it was their fault. Dad was my everything. He was really gone? I ran out of tears and my throat started to dry.

I went into the forest obliviously. I couldn't care anymore I started to run deep into the forest. It was already evening. I felt nothing and ran as my legs carried me away.

I ran and ran till I was so panting. I stopped as I saw a lake. Thousands of emotions and thoughts ran through my mind. I dropped down near the edge as I felt limp. "I'm so sorry, Dad," I fisted and hit the ground.

All I knew was that I didn't want to live anymore. I was so pathetic and useless. I had been a mess, a mess that threatened the beloved lives. My mere existence was a threat to them. I shouldn't have been born.

I never had a choice instead I was being told what to do... to obey my kidnapper... to submit..., including Mateo, Lizzy, or Sam.

I was so sick of all these shits. What more?

I got into the lake. The water wasn't shallow either. I was walking till the water level was under my chin. Oh yes, I couldn't swim. That Damien fucker abducted me while I was planning to learn swimming.

Every detail about my loss flashed to me as a movie. My life, my youth, my time, and my father? And what was next? My mother or my sister? I was chattering with coldness in the lake.

I felt all of my energies drowned with me as I let go of the very own lake floor that was providing me to float.

Coldness stroke my head and soon I felt the water was entering my lungs slowly and painfully. But no, this pain was nothing to be compared with what I was feeling right now.

It was like flying in space. I had no worries for now, at least. The very low air in my lungs completely left me giving me unbearable pain. I guessed now, it's time to say 'bye'

'Stay. Stay. Wake up.'

'Stay with me.'

'Vivan? Vivan?'

'Come on, breathe!'

I heard those voices. Was I in hell? I felt continuous pressure over my chest. It was hurt like hell.

The whole bulk of air entered my lung roughly bringing me back to life.

"Fucking breathe!!!!" I heard Mateo's voice booming through my eardrums. The water inside my lungs was thrown up as he held me sideways.

Damn...I was still alive then...

Then I felt a bone-crushing hug. Mateo cupped my face with his palms and kissed my forehead harshly.

"Thank god," Mateo said shaking lightly. He rubbed all over my back while letting my chin rest over his shoulder.

I was coughing water, furiously. Then I blacked out._________________

____

I felt the pain in my back as I started to wake up with a half-sleepiness. Mateo was carrying me in bridal style while walking with a straight look on his face.

"Put me down," I mumbled. He continued walking as if he couldn't hear me.

I reached out my hands to his jaw and pushed his head to the sideway. "Put me the fuck down," I seethed. That caught his attention. He only tightens his grip on my thigh not enough to hurt me but enough to keep me in place.

I tried to struggle but he didn't even pay attention to me.

I managed for him to put me down as I leaned in and bit down his chest hard. I pry off his hold and tried to get away from him as possible. But, my leg and back were betraying me.

Somehow, I managed to grab a hold of a tree and stood miserably. I glared at him and he was looking at me with an unknown expression but he quickly recovered with his straight face.

"Leave me alone!" I snapped at him.

He sighed and slowly approached me with his arms outstretched. I could see his pistol was tugged near his waistband.

I slowly back up to the tree and gulped as his stare made me uneasy. As he was about three feet away from me, I got the idea to distract him and grabbed the gun.

"What is that?" I said and pointed at his back. He turned around and I quickly snatched the gun from him. He was fast too but not as fast as me.

I was pointing at him with the gun. I didn't know how to use but somehow I saw how Damien shoot people around. Yea.

"You don't know how to use that, do you?" Mateo raised a brow.

I unlocked the safety and back off as he stepped a step.

He sighed and said, " of course, you do know,"

"Where's my mom?" I seethed.

"I saved your life and you're here threatening me?" He folded his hand.

"I won't hesitate to shoot you, Mateo. I've lost my father," I whispered.

Mateo furrowed his eyebrows and turned his back on me. "You don't know that for sure," he mumbled.

"Take me back to Damien. I'll kill him by myself," I snapped with determination in my soul.

"You know? He's- dammit.." he said and slowly turned around at me. "Calm down, okay?" He mumbled and tried to approach me again.

"Stay where you are or I will shoot your head," I threatened.

But he didn't listen and took intimidating steps at me. I screamed and reluctantly pulled the trigger.

"Bang!!!!!" A loud noise went off and I stumbled back with a hell of a pain in my hand. I doubted if my hand was broken already. The restrain was so strong.

Oh my god. Did I kill Mateo? I was panicking...

But, I knew...he missed that bullet the moment I felt the tight grip on my nape. He furiously inhaled as he observed my broken hands.

He quickly carried me in bridal style and took me into campus and laid me on the mattress. He was cursing under his breath and bandaged my injured hands.

I was sobbing so hard to the point of suffocation.

I looked at Mateo who was with a sad and angry expression on his face. He kneeled to my level and wiped my tears. I was surprised he didn't seem to care that I tried to kill him.

"Hush, " he said and placed his fingertip over my lips. I cried out more. Did he expect me to shut up???

"I-It h-hurts," I sobbed. Actually damn hurt.He ran his hand through his messy hair and got up grabbing a box. What he pulled out from the box made me freeze, a syringe.Fucking syringe!!!!!

"No, please, don't, " I mumbled with pleas.

"Hey, hey, Vivan, do you trust me?" He asked looking dead in my eyes.

However, he didn't wait for my reply and injected the syringe into my wrist despite my pleas.

"Believe me, breathe slowly," he said while rubbing my forehead.

Somehow his words affected me and I calmed down as I couldn't feel the pain anymore right now. I couldn't move my hands either.

Mateo suddenly got up and pulled out a handcuff quickly tugged my leg at a post. I struggled and looked at him with disbelief.

"I'll be back, okay?" He smiled and leaned forward. His breath fanned against mine as his lips softly landed on my cheek. It stayed momentarily but I couldn't stop the fluttering feeling in my abdomen.

With a short nod, he just walked out, leaving me alone in the tank, being tied........

The plethora of deceits had taken a toll on her sense of reality. Denial...anger...and confusion.

Chapter 29

----

(29)

"Did I regret?"

The question I had been asking myself for the hundredth time. My thoughts amplified with each repeat until the words didn't make sense anymore.

"Did I really think of drowning myself?"

Such a person, I was, would never be able to give answers because of that kind of person I had become. The old me wouldn't even think twice about doing such deed, but I did it.

As I linger on that thought, thinking about it, really thinking about it. " Did I really put myself at the death's door deliberately?"

"An orphan"

The one thing I feared the most. The one thing I had never expected to happen. I couldn't even bear the thought of it. I was alone and my sense of reality was fading. I wasn't not sure if I was really alive.

My hands were numbed and I couldn't feel my arms moving. I couldn't feel anything, not even pain.

It felt like forever when I saw Sam and Lizzy rushing towards my direction. Sam uncuffed my leg and carried me in bridal style as if they were in rush.

I laid my head onto Sam's chest as I was exhausted. Whatever, I needed to get back to Damien because he still has my mom. I wouldn't let him destroy the very last thing I have.

There came a car on the main road. The car window opened revealing Mateo. He said to Sam, " Set her beside me,"

Sam walked around the car and set me in the front seat. Mateo leaned in again so close to me but he only secured my seatbelt. He wasn't in a good mood as he tightened my seatbelt more than necessary as I glared at him groggily and he glared.right.back.at.me.

Mateo slammed the accelerator and drove off like a crazy man.

My mind was blank and I was more like in space. I could see many cars through the back mirror, so closely.

That's why he was driving like he wanted to kill us both. I covered my ears and shut my eyes tight. It was dark, wherever I was.

I knew I wasn't awake, although I wasn't sure how I knew that. Occasionally, visions appeared, lasting anywhere from seconds to hours. I had no sense of time anymore.

The voices were ringing nonstop in my head. I didn't know what happened but I learned the car has stopped and Mateo somehow managed to made the cars lost us.

We were still in the middle of nowhere. Mateo got out of the car and pulled me out as I was sitting like a corpse. I could feel my hands again now, and yet with pain. No words were exchanged as he dragged me by my uninjured hand till he reached his destination.

He let go of my hand and disappeared into a bush. But seconds later, he walked out with a motorbike. I couldn't help but impressed with how he had managed to keep up all the plans.

I shook my head in denial. What if Damien was planning one of his sick games? What if Damien deliberately letting us off the hook? Chasing had always been his favourite game.

But Sam and Lizzy were inside the car. I didn't bother to ask him about Sam and Lizzy. I simply couldn't care about them. Yea, that was me who had become. Helplessness and ignorance were gifted to me since I lost my own rights as a human.

Mateo started putting a thick jerkin on me that was twice my size. He zipped and made sure I was comfortable. Mateo motioned me to get on the bike. I did as he told me. Of course, I didn't have a choice.

He started the engine and told me to hold on tight. We rode for hours and hours.

Finally, the destination seemed to come. Mateo stopped the bike.

Everything was new to me...The people and the scenery felt awfully unfamiliar. He had stopped at a restaurant and started pulling me towards a corner and helped me take off the heavy jerkin.

After he made sure where people couldn't see us, he put on a hat and pulled the hoodie over my head.

After he was done with dressing me, he dragged me into the restaurant and told me to order something to eat. I just ordered a burger...

"Would you tell me what is actually going on?" I mumbled while sniffing at my burger.

Mateo's gaze falls upon me and he sighed but he didn't answer! I couldn't help but I felt the back of my eyes burnt and warm tears fell continuously.

"Don't fucking cry," he said pinching the bridge of his nose. With a snort he pushed his lemon juice towards me. I took a large gulp immediately and felt much better.

"Yea, I'm so sorry for crying over my dad's death. I'm so sorry," I whispered, "It's okay don't tell me anything until I find out my whole family death by myself. It was you tell me to trust you?" I snapped, but this time with anger.

"I thought you would help me. But you're doing nothing other than hiding and running. And you don't even want to tell me what the hell is going on!" I seethed. I knew my smart mouth was winning over him. I didn't care this was the last thing I had to try.

"It's not what you think. I'm helping you, Vivan," he said slowly. It was obvious he wasn't in the mood to answer me.

"You think you're helping me? Oh, so thankful. But You're. Not. Helping. Me. At. All!!! Why you're not telling me what was happening????!!!!" I snapped at him throwing the burger at his face.

With that his fist connected with the table making me jump. Some people's attentions were on us.

"Because it might be a fucking trap. And you're stupid to fall for his tricks," Mateo snapped at me. Trap? Oh my god. Then, dad was still alive?

"Trap? You mean dad might be still alive?" I whispered him with full of hope.

"I don't know. But I already told you, he wouldn't kill them if he wants you. I need you to trust me," he said rubbing his temple.

But it didn't make any sense. Why he just couldn't tell me that earlier? "How's my mom, then?" I asked.

"She would be fine," he mumbled. What was meant by that? With that he got up as his phone rang, he mouthed, " Don't move," I could see he was talking to the waitress to give me another burger.

But anticipation was killing me from the inside. I was genuinely happy and excited at the hope that my dad was still alive. But it also pushed me into vulnerability, I was feeling so much guilt for risking my parent's lives.

Mateo went outside through the back exist holding the phone so tight to his ears. I rushed behind him not so close but enough to hear him.

"She is being moved? Where? UCLA? Okay, I got it," Mateo mumbled. UCLA? UCLA? What the hell was that? What was meant by she? Who?

I quickly sprinted to my seat and asked the waitress," Umm. Excuse me. Does UCLA mean something?"

I was doing my best to avoid looking up at her face. Spending the whole week with Sam and Lizzy was helping me a lot not to cause my traumatic phobia.

"You mean UCLA medical center?" She asked with a raised brow. Medical care? I called her once again as she turned her heels to leave.

"Umm. Where am I now?" I asked.

That caught her attention. Damn. Stupid! Stupid, Vivan! You can't make her took an interest in you.

"California," she simply said and left me.

Mateo came back with a frown and stood Infront of me saying" Come on, let's go,"He then grabbed his coat.

I quickly slurred, " No! "

He cocked an eyebrow at my outburst "I mean, I wanna get some drinks,"

He nodded instantly placing the coat with the phone back on the table. He turned on his heel towards the counter. I quickly grabbed the phone but I found it locked.

'buzz' 'buzz' I almost choke on my spit when a call suddenly came in. I hesitantly accepted the call and... waited.

" The Martin's already in town, you need to get to Mrs.Kieran before they do," a familiar voice paused, "Hello, are you there, Mateo? "

I suddenly couldn't breathe. Everything started to fall into place. It must be her they're talking about, it must be Mom.

"Sam?"

"What? Is that you Vivan? Where's Mateo? Are you okay-"

"Sam, where's my mom? Tell me where she is. Please,"

"Vivan, calm down okay. Is Mateo still there with you? Are you alone?"

"Fuck you, Sam" I angrily pressed into the power button and watched it shut down.

I quickly put the phone back on the place and got up. I walked towards Mateo who was paying the cash. Everything felt like in a slow motion. Heavy and suffocating.

UCLA? That's why he couldn't face me to say about my mom. Thus why he kept off the subject.

I walked towards him and stood behind him. He turned around to face me with a frown. I wasn't sure what I would do but I snapped back into reality and said," I need to use the bathroom,"

His face softened as he nodded and said something to the waitress but I couldn't hear him. The waitress led me towards the back of the restaurant. I walked shakily.

Thus why he didn't say anything to me. He knew what I would do.

And he was right. I knew where my mom was. I was going to that hospital no matter what....

"Being blamed, defined, and deprived can impact anyone's confidence, expectations, characteristics, and aspirations."

Chapter 30

(30)I walked through the exit swiftly and sneaked out of the back of the restaurant as fast as my legs would carry me. I got rid off the excess clothing covering me to become less noticable and more casual.

I slumped against the thick trunk of the tree as my head momentarily fall back to rest against the rough bark. My legs shook and each breath burned in my throat. Shit. I'm really out of shape after those years spent sitting on my ass in a confined space. I strolled further down the road in hope of getting a taxi. But I realized I didn't get any money.

Double Shit!

I desperately tried to stop a car. Soon a car was pulling up, revealing an old couple with concern written all over their faces. 'Come on, Vivan. You need to use your acting skills now.'

"Is everything okay, dear?" The old man asked.

I took in a deep breath and let myself be consoled by tears. "My mom, she is in the hospital. And I lost my uncle here. I really need to go to the hospital, please," I sniffed but soon tears followed as I sobbed, " I don't have any money on me but I would be grateful-"

The old lady shushed me, "Oh my poor child, come with us. You shouldn't be alone, come quickly,"

By luck or by coincidence, I was on my way to my mom.

They dropped me off and I practically rushed towards the clerk. My ears were just ringing and I practically choked on my words as I forced myself to remain calm and recited my mom's name.

She gave me a look I couldn't quite decipher and pushed a pen in my direction. I impatiently scribbled my name and signature. She spat the room number and I was already on my heels, strolling down the busy corridor. I instinctively sucked my breath in as I digged my nails into my palms. 'Act normal, act normal.'

I looked down until I reached my destination. I hesitantly cracked the door open and the sight made me dizzy. The monitors beeping and my mother laying so lifeless on the bed but breathing ever softly. I struggled to keep my steps towards her steady. 'None of this should have happened'

I slowly reached to her fragile form. My fingers felt unfamiliar with the texture of her temple. It felt cold. She was always warm and at ease. Now I feel cold and tense. I gently eased my fingers in her hair, "Mom?"

I felt the muscles on my face tightening as I gripped on her palm. "Mom? Wake up!" I nudged her head with my own as if she would somehow complain me about the itchiness of my hair rubbing in her face. I nudged her shoulders to slowly shook her. 'Why won't she wake up?'

"Wake up,-" "Wake up,-" "Wake! up!"

She wasn't moving.

I longingly gazed at her chest rising and falling. I pull her palms against my cheek and for a while, I felt so safe.

I laid my head down the space and nudged her hand. She felt so cold. "It's all my fault. I'm sorry, mom."

My breath hitched as I snapped back at my back at the sound of door being click open. The sight made me froze, dad? Dad?????

He was holding a bag and staring at me as with his eyes wide as saucers. My legs were moving towards him unconsciously and found myself running into him.

I could feel the deafening heartbeats wilding in my ears as my body collided into his body.

Warm.

Familiar.

'Oh my god. Dad was still alive. Thank god. I'm sorry. It's all my fault.' I was saying gibberish at this point and dad's harsh grip on my face brought me back.

"-calm down, moonpie, breathe," a tear escaped from his soulful eyes and I was met with a sob followed by full blown cries that filled the room. It was an overwhelming feeling I couldn't suppress.

I was soon engulfed in his warm embrace. Dad's scent was the same, nothing has ever changed.

With a kiss on my forehead, he held my head between his palms while tears endlessly streaming down his face.

"Vivan. Is this you for real?" He heavily sobbed and pushed me into his embrace again. " Where have you been, all this time, my child? " His shaky voice shattered my heart into a million pieces.

I tightly held into his embrace... never wanting to let go of him.

"What happened to mom?" I was able to voice my thought after calming myself down.

With one heavy sob, I felt my world's fallen apart as Dad fell on his unsteady knees. The heaviness of my tongue aligned with the weight in my chest, I could only kneel down to his level and watch him sob hysterically.

"... cardiac arrest... after seeing the old videos of you. She kept saying it was her fault. I tried everything...moonpie. I tried everything in my willpower to find you, or to comfort the suffering of her soul, but it looks like ....I have failed," he shakily held out his hands.

I silently helped him up as he struggled to get up.

I guided him to properly sit down and stood up feeling numb as ever. 'Why did all of this happen?' I hang my head down in shame as I try to calm myself down. 'But what could I do? Now? How?'

"She is in stable condition now." Then silence fell upon again. I felt as though the walls are closing up on me. 'What should I do now?'

"Where have you been, Vivan?"

I was on the verge of crying again. I gulped thinking about the matters Damien had warned me. He said he didn't want me to expose anything particular about him or I would pay the price.

"I... I ran away...and there's a boy I really liked, so I ran away to be with him," I kept my gaze at Mom's pale face as I slowly formed the train of lies, " He rented us an apartment in that new neighborhood. He worked hard, he kept me safe, and he loved me. I ... I didn't expect it to be that hard to actually live by myself and someone I was in love when the one and only of my dependence never came home from work one day. I waited for two weeks all by myself with a cat that would probably be on the street by now," I took the sniffing sound as a cue to stop with the nonsense I've just said.

I had decided long ago to do anything in my will power to keep them in the dark for their own sake. I wouldn't risk them with the wretched fate of mine, I sure did start to believe I was cursed.

I flinched and gasped at the hand on my peripheral view, but quickly regained my posture as Dad's warm palm was placed on my cheek. His teary eyes wavering as he tried to contain his sobs in.

'You would never see me the same Dad, I'm sorry for everything, but I'll have to choose you two over myself,' I mentally recited.

I peeled his hand away as I turned my gaze back at Mom's shallow breathing.

"I am here to check in on Mom with a help of my friends, and I'll continue the search for him, because.... I can't lose him, I love him no matter what, so I'll be gone by the evening, I'm not coming...home...," I sucked in a breath as I anticipated about his reaction to my answer.

" Moonpie ..."

" Moonpie, look at me," Dad's voiced filled with concern as I kept my glare at the bedpost. I couldn't lie to him in his face.

" Moonpie... Please... ," I fidgeted on my clothes at his pleading voice, " Vivan... please,"

I wiped off the fat droplets of tears rather harshly as I stood up, " I'm gonna get some fresh air, I'll be back....." I stalked towards the door and swung it shut as I mumbled, " maybe I'll not...be back,"

I willed myself to keep taking leaps in an attempt to get away from the cries of a broken father.

Please forgive me.

'The possibilities, even if Damien barge in, would he dare to make a scene in a place like hospital?'

When I finally made it outside the hospital, I struggled to stand straight as I quickly scanned the surroundings before walking to the masked man on the motorbike not so far.

Mateo,... His demeanor changed as he put the phone away seemingly ending the phone call he had been making.

I stalked my way to him getting off the vehicle with heavy steps as I wiped the rushed tears. I watched him stood before me...emotions swirling in his eyes...I could help but jumped into his arms. I couldn't stop the shaking and started sobbing in his arms.

"Please, Mateo, take them with you and keep them safe. "

"No, Sam and Lizzy would be here any minute and we would rather die than let his claws on you again, you're coming with us," his heavy breath hit the top of my head as his grip tightened.

"Please-"

"No! I can't! I can't believe why would you ever think this as an option, Vivan, that bastard is sick-fuck. He had manipulated you into thinking you're responsible for your parents while he couldn't do shit,"

For a second, I felt hopelessness hit me. Damein had always been pulling his strings strategically. Early in the mornings, he was always suited getting ready for his work, not a hair out of the place. He must have held some reputation to keep, he wouldn't get his hands dirty anyhow. All this time... My life has been nothing but fallen deeper into his twisted vines. He was always one step ahead.

" He could be here any moment, right? " I said as a matter of fact.

"Vivan-" I cut him off. " Damien demanded you hand me over or he would hunt everyone down, right?"

Mateo's face showed no emotion as he looked away. Silence deafening.

" And you're not in the position to help me in any way because you couldn't step out of this state under his claws, am I fucking right, huh, Mateo?! " I couldn't stop the shaking as I cried my heart out.

Soon, my name was called after by Dad, as he came running towards me.

Dad approached me and pulled me away from Mateo. "Who are you? And what's going on here? " He stood before me completely covering me from the view as he puffed his chest with a strained voice.

I felt my heart broke a little more.

I needed to leave them...no I actually needed to get out of their lives...to keep them out of my own misery. It was my fate, maybe.

I understood how much this little time span should be cherished, just how much I may have taken for granted even if this would be the last time.

I silently tugged on Dad's shirt to keep his attention back on me.

" I'll find us a way out, I promise-"

I held out a hand for Mateo to stop. Suddenly realising the situation all too well, " I don't care why you're that much invested in this hopeless situation, Mateo, but I... I need you to do what's really necessary, "

His eyes filled with water as he looked at me, beyond insolace. He was devastated knowing what I had chosen and damn downright I wouldn't forgive him for what he had done.

Because it was Mateo Devins who had planned this out as to buy the time to smuggle me out of this country alone. He actually saw his sister and me as ones.

"Please take care of Mom and Dad,"----------------------

'It is to bite the bullet and doing this as the last wish I could ever ask for. If it would cost everything left of me to buy the time to distract that devil, I would do it in a heartbeat.'

I closed the door and sat down on the floor hugging my knees. The familiar feeling sank in as more tears burned through my eyes.

I was hyperventilating in an empty room, where I put up a fake bravado while walking Mom out of the hospital into the transfer ambulance, an hour ago.

It didn't take a fool to figure out where all these connections Mateo had, Lizzy Martin would be behind all of this. She surely must had unspoken histories with the ex-wife of Damien. And here I was a girl who happened to look just like that woman " Gabrielle Martin"

I felt used. They tried using me for their personal grudges against.... whatever the shit was... But they didn't seem to hesitate dragging my parents into this situation and using them as decoys to 'save' me.

I felt numb. I couldn't feel anything all of a sudden.

But... I could hear footsteps coming closer.

Soon after the footsteps were closer, I was pressed against the wall with a death grip on my wrists. That person was hovering over me with harsh assault on my lips and neck. I didn't need to know who it was, his brandy cologne proved that, Damien.

He pulled away and his minty breath brushed against my cheek. " Oh god, I missed you, did you miss me? "

My blood run cold at his dilated pupils. My body and mind went frigid and his hand went up to my neck holding with a tight grip. " Aren't you going to answer me, doll? " His voice muffled against my lips again.

I knew he was playing his sick games or else, he should be beating the shit out of me in any second. His grip was becoming tighter. I struggled to breathe. " Answer me. Uhhh. I hate it when you're like this doll, I really really really hate it, "

He suddenly let go of me and I crawled all the way back to the corner while trying my best to cover the area his leather belt would slash. I breathed through my nose as more tears rushed out and my vision blurred.

" Doll? "

" Doll, come here, "

" Doll, it's okay, it's not your fault, "

" Doll..."

" Doll! "

" Ughhh! Why?! Why?! Why?! Why can't you do the things I asked of you?!
"

" No... No... don't make me do this, doll. Not you, my doll, I won't let You
do this to me, "

Damien kept rambling nonsense which I supposed was the walls he had
been aiming his fists. His hunch-over figure emitted the blood thirsty vibe.
My lips started bleeding as I bit down hard to suppress my sobs. 'I'm scared,
Mom, Dad'

He had moved his attention back towards me.

He was clearly in his own head and the familiar emotionless gaze directed
towards me gave it all away.

'I'm going to be killed'

There he stood to his full intimidating height as he held out a gun.

Those atrocious and cunning gestures with a cruel claiming of the enam-
ored with that selcouth gore begged to differ from... Love.

How's everyone doing? The edited version will be continued weekly. Miss
you.

Chapter 31

----

(31)

    I couldn't realize what just happened until I felt the unbearable pain in my ears as a loud bang went off. A scream stuck in my throat and soon followed by heavy sobs as I felt a hard tug forced my face up.

"You missed me, right?"

Luckily the bullet did.

I could only huff a sob before the warm lips smacked against mine and soon followed by a tug on my hair that turned into a hard grip. I shuddered at the bruising tug as he pulled me up by the hair.

I tried not to give out any reaction to the burn of hot metal running along my cheek as he tightened his grip and trace patterns with the barrel of his gun. There was only a couple of time I had been cornered like this situation. Once or twice that i had the misfortune to witness that look in his eyes.

Soft spoken as if calm.Gentle as if kind.

He's definitely in an episode.

A loud phone call interrupted all my thoughts as I tried not to blink at his warning gaze.

'I need to keep his undivided attention to not risk him going after my parents. After all, it was me who has contacted him my exact location in the first place,'

I sniffled a sob as I felt his grip back on my throat as soon as he put his phone away. But I felt relief washing over me at the anger radiating of him as a good sign.

" Doll... " I felt him kiss the corner of my mouth.

" Where are they?"

I sharply inhaled at the sudden tightness of grip on my neck. He's asking about Mateo Devins.

" I- don- know " I crawled at his grip as i felt him pressing my temple at the gunpoint. I tried to look around as if any aid would help me.

" Look at me!" I could only whimper as I felt the familiar traumatic event came flashing before my eyes. 'Suddenly the room felt helplessly suffocating with the stranger man shouting me to finish the plate or he would shove it down my throat.'

" What does... he look like? " His eyes bore into mine.

I gritted at the realisation of him already figuring out as my expression gave it all away.

A scream ripped through my lungs followed by heavy sobs. My vision has gone blurry as unbearable pain shot up along with the unmistakable sound of my finger being broken. I could only bite down at the hand that was muffling any sounds from escaping.

" Shhhh, you weren't that talkative moments ago, "

'Mom, Dad, please make this stop,' I was hyperventilating at this point.

" Shhhhh "

" Shhhhh "

" Now, are you ready to talk? "

My voice faltering, " I- I'm sorry, "

He was processing my words, as he gave a subtle tilt of his head. For some moments, he stood so still that I thought the time has stopped.

A loud ringtone interrupted the moment as I tried to contained my sobs in.

The hard metal pressing against my temple was gone and I felt him bundle a handful of my hair by the roots again. His mouth descending on mine the same time I had gasped in pain.

I was out of breath by the time he stepped back and took the phone out facing away from me.

My legs gave up as I slid down to a kneeling position. ' Don't provoke him. Don't provoke him. Keep his attention. Keep his attention. '

Neither did I realize I felt the familiar stinginess on my cheek followed by a metallic taste of my blood nor did I comprehend that I was up in the air with my legs hanging freely.

" You're with that fucker! Huh! Out of all people you're with that little fucker?! Henry-fucking-Merlin again?!! " His words spewed out of his mouth but did little to me. I smiled at the realisation, ' he's going to end me and I have distracted him long enough, '

Before I was pushed into that darkness again, I was thrown onto the floor. Endless cough turned into laughters as I felt him shaking me. ' Merlin? Oh yea, it must have been his last name, my childhood friend who came back into town the day I encountered Damien, '

Although I had no idea how Henry's name was brought up into this, I chuckled at the irony of my own situation, but at least my parents are off this country for good. I trusted Mateo Devins to take care of them, now I thought I could only embrace my death, but Damien just have to be that much evil that he wouldn't just kill me off easily...

I felt him crouch down near me as I laid sideways.

I felt him lightly slapping my cheeks a few times before he demanded that I open my eyes and look at him.

I let out another bubbling cough mixed with giggles as I witnessed the unmistakable look of confusion written on his face.

" I- I- I hate you, "

With a sudden tug on my scalp, he pulled me up into sitting position as he leveled his eyes as a warning.

" I hate-"

Another slap but with the force that forced my head to the right.

I spat out blood mixed with my saliva as I let out uncontrollable babbling laughters.

" Go on, h- hit me again, go on! Kill me! I- I hate you, I- I hate you! " I gasped in pain as the weight of him suddenly crushed me on the floor. He had pinned me down onto the floor breathing heavily while I could only huff few breaths.

The silence on his side only encouraged me as I seethed in rage for all the things he had done to me, " You're someone I could never forgive even if you skin yourself alive, I hope you burn in hell, you're the one who is really pathetic, Damien. No one would ever...love someone like you! You evil bastard!! Kill me! Kill me! I hate you! I hate you! "

I felt his weight off me as I kept crawling backwards until I felt the wall on my back. The footsteps of him echoed in the room as he paced around muttering, ' shut up ' repeatedly as he smacked his palms on his head.

He fell on his knees as he kept smacking his hands on his head. He was talking to himself, this wasn't the first time.

" no, she doesn't mean it "" Lies, "" Not real,"" No, "" No, "" Don't hate me, "" Shut up, shut up, "

I mustered up the little energy I had and peered at my side where the window was. Two storey up height definitely would kill me if I fall head first.

" Lies, "" Not real,"" No, "

"Vivan! " I flinched at his strained voice as I stared at his shaking figure on his knees facing away from me.

" Please, no, no, don't hate me, " he kept repeating and his voice faltering with repeating words.

I palmed the walls as support as I desperate tried to reach the window.

" Not you, not you, baby, you don't mean it, "" Please, "" No, "

I felt the rush of cool air brushing my face as I successfully pulled the curtain out of the view and straddled the window sill.

" Doll?"

I gripped onto the curtains for support as I turned my attention back to him.

" Doll, come back down here right now, " his eyes filled with terror as he gazed me upward not moving an inch from his sitting position as if he was afraid of making a wrong move.

That's odd seeing that how he was always one step ahead and now he looked unprepared.

" Vivan, please, baby, "" No, no, you will not leave me! Vivan!"" No, fuck, baby. It's okay, please come to me, "" Vivan! I said come here! I'll fucking make you pay if you dare to attempt that stupid thing! "

" you're all I have... you're all I have"" You're all I have... You're all I have!"His tone dropped to whispering again before his gaze locked with mine.

I tightened my grip as he slowly but steadily offered his bloody palms open up but what I couldn't comprehend was how swiftly he had pulled out his gun and shot my left thigh.

I was screaming as my eyes rolled back towards my brains. My screams were soon muffled with the barrel shoved into my mouth. The agonising pain was taking over all my sense as I filtered out the swear words Damien was spewing before the barrel was removed from my throat.

I felt the back of my eyes burn at the painful death grip Damien had on my neck. Slowly but surely crushing my airways again.

Droplets of his tears splattered onto my face as I willingly slumped my muscles.

'Look who is crying now? '

Goodbye world.----------------------

Chapter 32

(32)

Suddenly all the air robbed out of my lungs as I was struck with familiar pain lacing each inches of my body. My heart-beat pounding in white noise was the only thing indicating I'm still...alive.

I can't see. I can't hear. I can't speak.

I could feel the blindfold secured over my eyes. I couldn't make any sounds past the particular increasing heartbeat of my own. I could feel the aching gag and the unfamiliar strap against my face, muffling over my mouth.

What the hell happened? Didn't I fall? I vaguely remembered that look of pure fear in Damien's eyes as he figured that his hand actually didn't quite reach me. In fact, I remembered that feeling... Calm. Yet confused.

I choked on my own spit when a voice that was too close too suddenly spoke, "How are you feeling?"

The piece in my mouth entirely rendered the useless words as I frantically tried to figure out if I was really dead. Was I in shock? The feeling of eyeballs moving was too real, the excruciating pain was too practical. Who? Who is it? Who was talking?

The piece covering my eyes were tugged off as I tried to adjust my eyes to the sudden light.

Grey eyes.

++++++++++++++

Daniel Martin's POV (Damien's twin brother)

I sighed a breath of relief at the change of the girl's breathing pattern because things had been building to this crescendos for awhile. It has been one ..no.. two years almost.

Things had been building and restarting the whole procedure at the same time.

Fair to the point, it had been from the smooth beginning of a childlike wish being fulfilled by that tense passion heat of a power imbalanced relationship.

Pushed to breaking and soon will...shatter.

"How are you feeling?" I sighed again at the sound of muffled voices. The events must have scared her somewhat.

I tugged off the blindfold and greeted by the fluttering of moist brown eyes. Only if those were ... something green- no. 'She's not her. And no. I don't give a damn knowing too well this is a literal declaration of war. The one I'm searching for is gone...'

" I'll take the gag off, and you're not to scream unless you want to alert my brother that you're awake, do you understand? " I explained the condition, considering her unstable state after near death experience.

I ignored the ache in my palms as I eyed the too tight strap marks on the soft skin being pinched. Except the eyes...even the defined cupid bow of lips- no. No!

" Do you remember what happened? " I grabbed her chin to tilt her head up so I could see in fact this girl..this prisoner of my brother was not ' HER '

The gradual blinking turned into a hard edge glare.

There was it.

I wanted to see her spark, to know what it looked like, so that when the circumstances crushed the rebellion out of her, I would see it in her eyes.

An expectation of something coming out of this interaction of going against the rules was apparent, even if I actually had no way to define the feeling, but it came in a way I least expected.

Despite the lack of violence in the motion, such reaction was expected of her.

Still sparks of rebellion swirling in depths of the grimness of determination. She remained silent, suspicion clear in her widened eyes.

" I'll ask again. Do you remember what happened? If yes, good. If not, I'm afraid I'm not in the place to tell you just that. "

Again I ignored the ghosty feeling of running the pad of my thumb over the flushed lips, tracing along the features.

'She had every intention of surviving the entirety. Fire, practicality, and hope blended together. She would be difficult to break. So familiar yet so distant.'

After another moment, I released her and stood back up. " I'm not in any position to sympathize you if you ever wonder why, " I queried as I turned my back on her and reached for the syringe on the table.

'just like my brother...no... it's fate. The history is repeating itself in the hands of the unfortunate. Really.. twins are bad luck.'

With a few coughs and sharp intake of breath, a whisper break through my thoughts. " Water, ple-ase,"...I realised I spaced out a bit as I grabbed the long forgotten pill with the glass of water. I turned to her with a grin, " there they always say the younger twins are evil, really now?"

+++++++++++++

Vivan Kieran

The twin kept coming up with occasional questions and some skittles of muffled thoughts.

I could hear him very well but my mind was practically searing with un-concealed rage as I watched his expressions. Why? Maybe because if I were to do that to the other twin, I wouldn't be off the hook with this same glint of excitement in such pair of grey eyes, and faint touches on my face.

Maybe because I anticipated the nonexistent future I had imagined for myself when I learnt I might've actually died.

Maybe because I felt this little act of rebellion wouldn't have conse-quences?

I watched him turn away from me, and throw his head back in the same posture Damien sometimes does when he couldn't sleep in the middle of the night. It had only been a few times I had seen the posture because Damien had always been extra careful when he didn't want me to wake up from him leaving the bed.

And although rarely, sometimes it led to the soft tuggings to wake me up and pull me onto his lap only to marr my skin with his teeth until I was a sobbing mess, begging him to let me sleep.

I kept my eyes on Daniel's back as I struggled wiggle my body even a bit.

I was restraint. I couldn't move..at all.

I struggled to get my throat working,"Water, ple-ase,"

I cringed at the grin he gave when he turned around. Suddenly I felt my heart trembling at the reality I was in. The reality that Damien would barge though any door anyhow right now or later.

" there they always say the younger twins are evil, really now?"

Younger?

Another unsolicited information? I guess...

The sound of footsteps echoing through the dungeon hallways had me rolling my eyes backwards, the noise too traumatic to actually get myself to accept that I actually didn't die and in fact, the very last second I thought I was going to die, ...I regretted it...I want to live.

I actually didn't want to die. Maybe it wasn't so bad that I was the one who was fking up everything in my head? Couldn't I just actually get used to being pushed around and manhandled??

The door swung open and my breath hitched at the smell of whisky and colonge hit the room in full wave. 'This is bad. Drunk Damien is another level of unpredictable shIt.'

My body acted as if on autopilot as I tried to remain calm but to no avail as I couldn't contain the terrified sobs at the feeling of a body hovering over mine.

There it was. Grey eyes.

bored into mine. Those were almost shining in dim light. Those were his tears?

I flinched at his hand but it was a glass he was holding. He held the glass to his mouth and shot up. He didn't gulp down but instead he forcefully connected his mouth to my own and passed the fluids right into mine. I could feel the fluid spilling down out of my mouth rolling down my neck as I tried not to swallow too much.

The furious yanking my hair had me whimpering. I had to gulp the liquid. But not for long, I puked back all way out.

I glared at him with so much hatred and yet this much dread and fear for him... from the bottom of my heart. He cocked his head sideways in a psychotic way making my stomach twisted in dread.

What the heck he was planning?

"You need to drink this," he slurred rubbing the glass against my cheek.

I breathed in and out slowly. 'Don't provoke him.'

" Why would I need to drink this?" I countered as I watched his expressions.

He grinned at me. Pure evil.

" I don't want to," I shattered with fear.

But his face suddenly fell. It didn't matter I realised the look of determination for whatever the sick plan he had up his sleeves.

He pulled out a sliver little knife from his pocket.

This was too soon... this was too soon.

He placed that shiny thing over my uninjured thigh and held the glass against my lips again.

" Why?" I asked reluctantly. A thing or two I had learnt it was never wise to deliberately try to give him silent treatment. Because I had dealt with those eyes glazing over listening to whatever imaginary voices he had back there.

He got up and come back with another mouthful again to force the burning, bitter, unpleasant liquid into my throat.

Of course, he successfully made it. When I was about to puke he shut my mouth with his hand shushing me to calm and gulp down like ' a good girl.'

I was feeling light-headed and hiccuped a few times. " Why?" I slurred out.

"Because of this," his voice so low and the next thing I knew was a sharp pain over my thigh. He was cutting my flesh with that damn knife. I screamed at top of my lungs.

He laughed like a maniac and roughly shoved something into my flesh.

I was struggling like a wild animal while trying not to black out. He would kill me..he actually would because..

"Ughhhhh!!!!!!" I screamed out as he poured down the remaining whiskey over my thigh.

.. because he was the one who pushed me off in the first place......

Note : sorry for the late update, I actually lost track of time after going on hiking trip with my friends. I'll be back on with another one as soon as I can.

Anime update- I've finished Hunterxhunter , damn that anime is almost top tier with AOT, I loved every single character of it.

Chapter 33

----

(33)

I was currently moping in the corner.

When I woke up this morning, Damien had left, sticking a note in my palm.

=================================" I'll be back at 5.Finish your meals along with the meds.Don't mess with the bandages.

See you, doll."===================================

I sighed and crushed the note into pieces.

I scooted into the bathtub filled with warm water, I guessed Damien prepared that for me since it was already lukewarm.

As soon as the warm water consumed me, I was relaxed. I peeled off the bandages and saw the wounds were almost gone.That was pretty impressive that a gunshot wound was gone just in about a week. What on Earth with the injections he's been giving me?

Of course, Daniel was forcing me to take those injections every day.I lay in the bed tub, lost in thoughts. A sudden wave of pain in my heart formed at the thought of Mateo. But why? I had nothing to do with him.

But he helped me with his life on line? I don't get it at all. What even is his purpose?I doubted if he was still even alive.

Damien was keeping a stoic face at my refusal to speak any further about my time while I was away with his sister in the woods. He didn't even brought it up. But I know better...

A monster would remain a monster no matter what. Something is up. Something is up his sleeve.

I shooed away the maids as they wouldn't go anywhere but stuck to me like freaking worms. I made sure I was alone in the room.

I stood in front of a full-length mirror and stripped down my clothes until I was completely naked.

Yea, my body was healing slowly but the fainted scars were everywhere.

Especially on my back where Damien used to beat with a leather belt, that belt was his favorite, but he used that only when I pushed his buttons and his sick mind overwhelmed him. Freaking psycho rat bastard.

My face scrunched in terror as the memories flooded again. The sight of tattoo was pushing me to the edge of insanity.

"Cling. Cling." The phone rang off, the phone that was only able to receive the incoming calls of course.

I lazily picked it up and held it into my ears. It felt cold against my cheek but nothing compared to the coldness that swallowed my fingers.

" Miss me, doll?" An amused voice.He usually didn't make calls unless it was necessary. Or to tick me off.

"With every bullet so far," I replied.

He chuckled and said, " So sassy when she wakes up..." he laughed.

" Just leave me alone," I seethed.

" Oh, doll, I wished I could but the show is fucking great!" I had to pull the phone away from my ear at the high pitched voice. The fUck? He sounds like the run down

I furrowed my eyes and sighed.What was this time?

" I still couldn't believe a little girl like you got so fucking sexy curves," he cooed.

What the heck he was saying? Verbal assaults as usual?But wait, he said the show was great and about curves...

I quickly grabbed the towel and wrapped it around me.

Mother fucker has already fixed the cameras in this fucking room. I could hear another squeaking laughter from the line." Oh, my smart girl. But you know, you're too naive sometimes," he chuckled." Go eat breakfast after you done with your little show...and don't you wanna count me in while you're at it- " he started moaning. What the-

Ugh.

I dumfoundedly stared at the wall in silence until he breathlessly called me out one last time.

The line went silent for a while.

I heard him sigh deeply." See you later, doll. I have to continue asking your little friend where did he hide your parents," he chuckled darkly and I heard some groans before he hangs off quickly.

What the heck????!!!! Did he mean Mateo?I knew it! Damien wasn't that generous and stupid to leave my parents alone!!

The blood was streaming down from my knuckles with shattered glasses deeply sticking into my knuckles as I keep pushing into it.

The mirror no longer showing my reflection

(Evening)

I tired myself off after crying.

My blood was drying off so far but the maids only came inside to clean the mess.I sat down on the wet floor in the bathroom and washed my hand sniffing and looking down at my blood-stained white gown.

Damien would be here in a minute as I could hear the car being pulled up.

I heard things being broken downstairs.Oh great, Vivan. You were fucked up now.The moment he mentioned hurting or anything about my parents I couldn't remember much after that.

Damien stormed into the room with his heavy steps. I only focused on washing my hands. I knew he was standing at the entrance as his heavy breath was vibrating.

I looked up at him as he was silently standing there for more than five minutes.His face held confusion and anger.His gaze turned between my hand, my bottom, and my eyes, and he licked his lips.

" Give me a good reason not to drag you out of there and spank that tight ass of yours,"

What?? Did he not just say that? He would beat the shit out of me if I tried any kind of self-harm before, but what was holding him back?

......

"You're acting like this ungrateful little bitch just so you can finally get me to give my sole attention on you huh?" He continued to accuse me.

" you want Daddy's attention, aren't you, doll? look at you... can't go a second without me." His voice low as tightened his grip on my throat.

Digging my nails at his wrists become my salvation as he kept gripping harder when I push at his chest.

I squirmed underneath his body as the water keep filling up the tub.

" Shh. " Water from his partially curled hair dripped on my face as he hovered above me. My back hurting from the crushing weight above me. My sensory was overloaded as he kept biting and bruising around the corner of my mouth. Gasping for a breath of air become too overwhelming it basically was him granting me a puff of breath only when he felt like it.

That goes on for another five more minutes.

I began feeling like I was a floating rock. But I could feel the grip on my neck also becoming looser as I zoned out and my limbs going weak.

He let me go with a quick kiss to my numb lips where I sat up and greedily inhaled sharply until falling into a coughing spur, throat tight and itchy with burning for air.

"Giving up already? How about we take a break? " I felt him feeling up my breasts as he snickered.

I gathered the spit in my mouth to spit at him. But the look in his eyes caught me off guard, his eyes are ... Red....it must be from water going into his eyes right? There's no way he would f-cking cry-

I saw the lone tear spilling down his right eye as he stared at the wall behind me. He didn't even seem like he's here.

As he shifted his gaze on me...and I knew...

———————————

The familiar pain spreading through my wet tousled locks as I gritted my teeth keeping myself from screaming again.As if on cue, the pulling becomes unbearable as he yanked me up and keep my head in place.

A yelp caught in my throat as I was bounced on the bed with him straddling me.

I gripped the sheets and tried pulling myself away from him. With a tug on my ankle, he flipped me face down into the sheet as he trapped me beneath him using both of his grips in my hair and my wrists.

My vision becoming blurry as I felt him trying to restrict my movement to nothing by just laying on top of me.

" I know you liked that bastard," I felt his breath directly on the back of my head.

" Don't you, huh? He is your f-cking superman, " his accusing tone had me biting back my tongue. " Fucking admit it, you little whore!!!" His nails were digging into my flesh.

I sobbed in pain."No,"

Suddenly I was flipped back onto my back. I felt his cold palm stroking me painstakingly gentle. " You like me better right? Right?" I felt him licking my nose. Yuck. I grimaced as I felt his fingers prodding my closed eyelids.

" I'm better right? "

And so the endless circle repeats.________________

Third person POV -

The fabric of her shirt was strained beyond its limits in his tightly clutched grasp, as he shoved her with great force back into the open doorway of the building.

She hit the cold tile floor with force, her hands and knees landing first before catching herself on her shins to prevent a potentially dangerous fall.

The sudden sound of the door slamming shut echoed in the empty corridor.

He took a brutal grip on her upper arm with his large and rough hand, and forcefully yanked her upright, dragging her along at a pace that proved too quick for her to keep up. She stumbled and stumbled, struggling to stay upright and on her feet as she was dragged forward by his relentless grip.

She attempted to kick and squirm within his relentless grip, but her small sobs proved insufficient in freeing herself from his grasp, her skin beginning to burn as he continued to tightly twist his grip, not letting go of her even as she continued her desperate attempts to free herself.

But he seemed unbothered, eerily so, almost as though he was doing something as mundane as carrying in groceries, a sack of potatoes and not a distressed little girl.

Completely nonchalant as his dark curls, wet, laid slick and dripping over his eyes where he held an almost deadly calm stare on ahead of him.

To the basement it was...

____

I couldn't even feel my legs as I was dragged alongside.

He growled loudly and yanked my hair more aggressively, dragging me along the way. I was practically running to keep his pace because I didn't want to be dragged along.And his long strides weren't helping me at all.

" You dare to say 'no' to me? Am I not enough for you? You of all people?!" He seethed while dragging me towards the basement. " My f-cking property?! " he snapped angrily at my face.

I guessed he reached his destination as he threw me onto the cement floor. I looked up and saw a beaten-up, Mateo. Yes, I had nothing to do with him but- but- he helped me to meet my parents again. My head is spinning like crazy. It really was him whimpering.

The wave of guilt strokes me hard like lightning.

But Damien again held the back of my head and forced my head up making me look at Mateo.

The mere idea of Damien forcing me to watch him possibly end Mateo caused me to shut my eyes tightly and break out into tears. The terror of such a scenario occurring gripped me, leaving me overwhelmed and fearful of the possibility that such an event could transpire again.

"Open your fucking eyes!!!!" Damien placed a plier inside my palm. Wait, a plier?

" Are you sure you don't wanna play the game?" Damien breathed into the back of my head making me shiver.

"N-No! Just kill me a-already!" I sobbed as the mental and the physical burden was too much for me to handle.

"Wrong answer," he mumbled and I felt him gripping my hand tight with the device.

The next thing I knew was a loud, painful, unpleasant groan from Mateo.

I was logged out lol.Been like five months aye.Some of you damn supportive I love it... Dedicated to those who has been requesting.

Chapter 34 part 1

---

3 4 part 1

I tried to retract my hand back but Damien had other plans with his bruising grip on my wrist.

I couldn't force myself to open my eyes as Mateo's anguished whimpers left no doubt as to his immense suffering.

A rough grip on my nape forced a strangled whimper. His breath fanned against my ear."Look what you made me do to him,"I knew I would regret opening my eyes but I did it.

Oh my god... Damien had cut his.... little toe.

Or Did I do it? I managed to get his grip off my wrist as the blood was making it extremely slippery.

A terrifying sight of blood followed the severing of a little toe.Blood was all over the place.

I threw up everything in my stomach and tried to crawl backwards as I struggled to catch my breath and deal with the lingering nausea.

"Now, he is going to die if you refused to play the game, " Damien said with a calm tone.

Damien's wrath was utterly justified, as I'd tried and failed to flee his grasp for an entire year. In the preliminary stages of my escapes, he'd always resort to physically battering me.

But this time? I escaped.. like really, I successfully fled from Damien, remaining away from him for a full two weeks.

The scars adorning his wrists were testament to his ...whatever you call it...during my absence, with him picking at his skin in his distress. Furthermore, subtle display of rare humanlike behavior whilst maintaining his trademark blank, expressionless gaze is truly unsettling.

'psychopath'

"Yes or ...yes?" He mumbled. I couldn't see him but I could hear the smirk in his statement-like question.

The temperature seemed to go down a degree as I tried my best to stop the tears. Everything was blurry and the dim light bulb in this soundproof basement wasn't helping.

He didn't even turn to look at me as he continued to examine the toe he just made me cut.. it was sickening sight to see...

"So I'm getting the silent treatment?!" His tone going a bit low as I remained quiet.

My hands growing numb from trying to crawl further away from him.

"Hm..."

'you would hurt me anyways!' I waited with a bated breath as I thought to myself.

"I can't read minds you know?"

A hitch in my breath interrupted my thoughts as he suddenly reached for the pliers, turning towards me with a menacing look in his eye.

Unflinching in the face of my cries, he firmly seized my right hand and I struggled like a wild animal.

"I don't read minds, but I know when little brats like you try and revolt against the hands that feed you, aka me!"

It only became worse when I heard the crack, followed by excruciating pain flooding through me. With him letting my hand go, I crumpled to the floor.

The awkward angle my finger was currently at confirmed the truth; it was, indeed, somewhat broken.

Fretting over my broken finger was not an option as my adrenaline continued to soar. That was my worst nightmare about to become a reality—my limbs being lopped off. My body began to shake due to such an awful notion.

"Damien, P-Please... please..." Releasing a weak whimper and adopting a defeated expression, my sense of hopelessness took hold.

Trying not to flinch at him approaching and abruptly grabbed me by my throat only to assault my mouth. He sucked the life out of me while gripping my windpipe.

He habitually relied on that habit to pacify himself. Tilting my head to meet his eyes after planting a harsh kiss on my forehead.

"I guessed that's a yes," not a question...

I nodded exhaustedly.

An unsettling smile, given the dreadful set of circumstances I was facing, appeared on his face. Leading to him dragging me out of the basement and impatiently carrying me upstairs.

My eyes struggling to adjust the light outside.

I knew there's no going back at the revelation of his movements practically giving the unhinged vibe.He put a cloth over my eyes and knotted behind my head swiftly.I could sense he was excited or happy as his hands were shaking.

I felt the cold wind stroke me.

He quickly removed the cloth when he reached his destination.

I sure was outside...and it was backyards opposite from the gates I've trying to pass through.

I was facing the forest, a large one at that.

I dared to take a peak back at him... him already aiming a gun at me.

" Run."

Yo!

The updates are erratic I know!But I've got more chapters to edit and much less time to do it because I have been working.

This book has 100+ chapters and I'm going to continue it after updating the remaining 35-90.

Book 2 will be confusing if you're a new reader because chapters between 35-99 were being taken down.

It's exhausting I know...but I think I'll be updating more frequently from a month now on.

Luv ya, I'm just busy...not dead

Chapter 34 part 2
Damien's pov

3 4 part 2 special chapter

Damien Martin's POV

(The flashback when Vivan got her period)

"It appears that my girl has finally entered into womanhood. Her menstrual cycle has begun, marking the conclusion of her transformation into an ideal companion. She will slowly but surely learn to adapt to the life ahead of her.."

I want to provide her with more freedom, such as giving her treats other than some silly chocolate privilege. I feel as though I should be more lenient with her.

"This is a common symptom of that particular physiological state, as the frequent fluctuations in her hormonal levels can cause intense emotional instability." I recalled my brother's words.

No wonder she's moody about everything little thing.

Her resentment towards me is at an all-time high right now, but I find it nothing but pathetic attempt at being a revolting brat to give Me a taste of her frustration.

Her circumstances literally entail spending the remainder of her life with me without a doubt.

————————

(The day Vivan was allowed to see her family again)

Her heart-rending weeping and her downbeat stare at the car window was the only thing seemed alive yet so broken.

Initially, when I brought her to this location, she attempted to flee on given chance. Hence, I resolved to be on increased alert and follow her every maneuver with meticulous attention.

That moment seeing her crying over her family, I felt the rage bubbling inside me. That brat...She must smile and cry, for me only.

The sole thing holding me back from forcing her to return to the inn was her unceasing whimpering and trembling, with her slim frame, as she cried uncontrollably. 'She's BeAuTiFuL like this.'

Afterwards, I led her to this flower field, where she had the time of her life. She even managed to give me a faint smile.'Such a confusing little thing.'

I spent my miserable ten years while I saw Gabrielle's face everywhere.

But now I was looking at Vivan, I saw Vivan, only Vivan. Vivan was the only one who could make me forget about any other things this world present to me.

Ever since my birth, everything was handed to me, yet I owned nothing, a contradiction that is deeply ingrained in my being even now.

'I felt her tensing up as I get closer to her to take a look at the flower bundle she's been making.'But this... this complete control over something.. something that I solely own is exhilarating.

Eyes never lie.

I couldn't understand how that girl could be so happy and carefree even after me having subjected her to such atrocities.My brain struggled, attempting to fathom it. How was that girl, despite her suffering at my hands, still able to be joyful and carefree? I was left puzzled and mystified by the matter.

'I trailed my fingers across her bottom lip as she seemed to be wanting to be somewhere other than sitting with her captor as she tightly gripped onto the flower bundle.'

A look without needing much words. She reluctantly leaned in to give me a kiss on the cheek.

Smart choice.

I leaned on the car and lost in my thoughts with a cigarette while I let her enjoy her little exploration.

I wouldn't make the same mistake again,Those memories haunted me like a shadow.

A decade back, Gabrielle was something akin to a blessing for me. Something I could call as my own thing.

But I couldn't fathom why I would have made the mistake of letting her walk all over me. That was what love means right?

I had the option to do away with her, yet I didn't have the heart (or the means)... the man who I call father was set on wanting a heir from me.

I was young.

The possibility of her abandoning me on my own with our shared off-spring in tow was what truly haunted my dreams.How...how could I possibly protect the young from the destiny that has been projecting from me?

No child, I mean no child deserves to be abandoned by their birth mother. My child would be no exception too.. that child wouldn't be more cursed having me as a father.

So I take on a whole new persona. Turning out to be the worst. I was a teen at that time, being taught like a true bastard who has no morals by my very own father, and my childhood trauma blinded me. I thought she would pity and LoVe me if I were to play along...PiTy? LoVe?

.....

'I looked down at the bundle of wild flowers presented to me.' The past is in the past.

I lost everything since then.

'The fidgeting hands reached out to present another bundle she has hidden behind her back.' This is my new reality.

'The savory taste of her lips never fail to amaze me as she dug her nails into my hands that's pulling on her scalp a little too tight.' Such a refreshing... little thing, how could I ever let you go?

Sleep, drunk, sitting in a room of masked people with the bastard I call father.

Daniel, my twin brother, had assisted me in recovering from severe alcoholism. Our father had made us all believe that Daniel perished at a tender age due to cancer, but this turned out to be a ploy concocted by our evil father to execute his devious schemes. Nevertheless, my brother was there to support me, aiding my recovery from rampant alcoholism. Afterward, he left me to pursue a career in medicine, abandoning me to my own devices.

It wasn't until that abhorrent individual, whom I referred to as my father, finally took his life by a gun he used on my mother. I was granted a measure of respite from his reign of torment.

Served the bastard right.

I recommended working, this time as a replica of Daniel since I needed to conceal all evidence pertaining to him. The nightmares, however, persisted with me having to swallow numerous sedatives each day to stay functional. I didn't even know why I was alive.

On a given day, I caught a glimpse of the cafeteria while driving by, and my heart skipped a beat.

I saw Gabrielle...I quickly retracted the car and took a closer look, but it wasn't Gabrielle but a strikingly similar lady.

Despite knowing the ethical implications, I couldn't turn my attention elsewhere even if I endeavored to, transfixed on her beautiful visage that was all too captivating to me, even at a distance.

Too...young.

My life was all predetermined from the moment of my birth--even my father would often chastise me for not being appreciative of the path that was set in stone for me from the very first day.

Yet, I had no true yearning or genuine goals for myself until this particular day, for the first time ever. That was all a result of the overpowering emotions that were urging me to .....

Capture?

Protect?

Eradicate?

I felt as though I had no other choice but to follow my impulse.

I began to trail after her, scheming how I might interact with her without appearing peculiar.

But that plan long forgotten as I blinked and then my hands were covered in blood of a boy trying to kiss my... my....my Thing... That empty feeling and trauma coming full force on how people seemed to can't keep hands off Things I Own!

Not anymore.

With my vision blurry and all, but my mind was clearly set on getting my hands on that wide-eyed pretty little thing looking up at me with so much horror.

Addicted.

Pretty things attract attention...Even the people I hired to take care of her basic needs seemed to grown attached to her, and henced leading me to practically go extra length to ... hire people under my father's. They would know better than to step out of line.

Which was a desperate attempt on the surface but works wonder with how I didn't have to bloody my hands on minor circumstances.

(Damien went to check on Vivan's mother who went into heart attack)

Turned out as my worst nightmare. It ultimately appeared to come true, for a call notified me that a mob had snatched Vivan into their possession.

In a frenzied state, I rushed back to the inn as I drove like a lunatic, only to discover that my hired goons had been brutally assaulted.

Everything I held dear became airborne, followed by destruction at my own hands. I held myself responsible; was I to be deemed a failure yet again? I raged in a torrent of self-loathing. A failure again???!!!________________

I was so consumed by my anguish that I never took a bath or consumed any meals, relying solely on consuming whiskey to assuage my sadness. I spent all of my waking hours awaiting for my cell phone to ring. If the abductors were simply seeking money as ransom for her release, they no doubt would have contacted me by now to make a monetary exchange.

But how was this even possible? Vivan wasn't even being seen by anyone... I kept her tightly hidden.

Yet, it was utterly baffling--I always had Vivan safely stored out of the public's sight. It was incomprehensible to fathom how the kidnappers had the wherewithal--or the opportunity--to even take her from me in the first place.She's a literal ghost since I've taken care of the records.

'Fuck!!!" I smashed the bottle against my head. Blood was dripping down my face but the pain was nothing compared to the nothingness in my heart.

No person aside from that imbecile of a sister, whom I'd believed I could count on, had knowledge of Vivan's presence.

The shocking revelation that she and her pathetic excuse of a husband went missing a week ago had not returned was the most suspicious aspect of all.

Pretty things really do attract AtteNtion.________________

Setting up a fake death plan was a child's play. I put up three locations in case...

And sooner,'A call from an unknown ID.'

So the old clothes of her father's worked wonders.

Little sob and heavy breathing. GUILTY.

"Hello, my love." But then the line was dead but I already got the location.

"Daniel, I need your help."

My fury was palpable--what sort of incompetent goons were these that they'd failed to obtain her?! However, it seemed that my sister and her husband weren't the only individuals with a vested interest in this matter; someone else was most certainly involved.

I paced about my house like a deranged man, becoming increasingly agitated by the passing of time. Being separated from her for almost two weeks was a true living nightmare for me.

I tricked Vivan's simple-minded father into signing the documents to permit her mother's transfer to UCLA under the false pretense of governmental aid. I had no qualms about hurting Vivan's emotions, as my desperation to be reunited with her was paramount over everything else.

I   wouldn't   chase   her.She   would   come   to   me.
______________________________(Refer to chapter 30)

Soft ... delicate... delicious... such a precious thing trembling at the sight of me. My rage could even melt if this little thing were to reciprocate my affections. I was whipped.

" Oh god, I missed you, did you miss me? "

WIDE EYED.

" Aren't you going to answer me, doll? "

FREEZING LIPS.

" Answer me. Uhhh. I hate it when you're like this doll, I really really really hate it. "

CURLED UP IN THE CORNER YET NO HINT OF REGRET IN FIREY EYES.BUT THIS...THIS LITTLE THING IS TERRIFIED AT THE SAME TIME.

" Doll? "

" Doll, come here, "

" Doll, it's okay, it's not your fault, "

" Doll..."

" Doll! "

" Ughhh! Why?! Why?! Why?! Why can't you do the things I asked of you?! "

" No... No... don't make me do this, doll. Not you, my doll, I won't let You do this to me, "

UNGRATEFUL.

I pulled out a gun.

An act of defiance.And a SCREAM.

"You missed me, right?"

The sheer beauty that appeared in her eyes as she gazed upon the metal hovering above her skin.

Soon a phone call, informing that this little devil had indeed went out of her way to ensure her parents safety.

" Doll... "

LITTLE DEVIL.

" Where are they?"

LIES. BETRAYAL. The AUDACITY.

" Look at me!"

" What does... he look like? "

NEVER RECALLED TEACHING HER TO BE A SLUT.

A broken finger would heal nicely if fractured in the right way.

" Shhhh, you weren't that talkative moments ago, "

THE PARENTS YOU LOVE ISN'T COMING TO SAVE YOU.

" Shhhhh "

" Shhhhh "

" Now, are you ready to talk? "

NO YOU'RE NOT SORRY.

Another phone call informing there was indeed a man involved in schemes of my sister.

" You're with that fucker! Huh! Out of all people you're with that little fucker?! Henry-fucking-Merlin again?!! "

CONCUSSION? IF NOT WHY THE SUDDEN LAUGHTER?

I didn't hit her that hard.

'IHAtEYoU'

DON'T YOU DARE BRAT.

" IHAte-"

SUCH VENOMOUS MOUTH BE DAMNED.LAUGHTER AGAIN.

" Go on, h- ****hit me again, go on! Kill me! I- I h*** you, I- I h*** you! "

FURY BLINDING. Disrespectful.

" You're someone I could never forgive even if you skin yourself alive, I hope you burn in hell, you're the one who is really pathetic, Damien. No one would ever...love someone like you! You evil bastard!! Kill me! Kill me! I h*** you! I h*** you! "

SHUT UP. SHUT UP. SHUT UP.

" no, she doesn't mean it "" Lies, "" Not real,"" No, "" No, "" Don't hate me, "" Shut up, shut up, "" Lies, "" Not real,"" No, "

"Vivan! "

" Please, no, no, don't hate me, "

" Not you, not you, baby, you don't mean it, "" Please, "" No, "

WHERE IS SHE?

" Doll?"

IT'S DANGEROUS. WHAT IS SHE PLANNING ON DOING?

" Doll, come back down here right now, "

" Vivan, please, baby, "" No, no, you will not leave me! Vivan!"" No, fuck, baby. It's okay, please come to me, "" Vivan! I said come here! I'll fucking make you pay if you dare to attempt that stupid thing! "

" you're all I have... you're all I have"" You're all I have... You're all I have!"

CONFESSION.

How.... how ... how ... dare YOU reject me.

ONE SHOT AND... THE REST IS BLURRY.

She won't get away. Not even by death.---------------------A raw slice to the perfect skin on her thigh spluttering with generous blood and so were the screams that followed. A TRACKER FOR A LESSON LEARNT.

Just a taste of what I'm truly capable of...yet, the little thing shivering and derilious with silly flu.

WEAK.

Kissing goodbye to the sweat covered forehead before leaving for work make me feel beyond content. Bruises and mark.

ART._________________

(After being informed that the man involved was no one other than Gabrielle's brother Mateo)

I was shocked. No. It would be an understatement. I was beyond livid. How dare he show his face.

And the little devil? Sure as fuck would be in her silly world of Romeo and Juliet. Sorry but that's going to work. Because I had plans concerning finding some fucker who looks exactly like Mateo.

Specifically because brats like her who were being trained in the dark basement on a weekly basis would struggle to remember their own faces.

WOULD BE FUN.

Because little spice wouldn't be able to handle something a little too graphic.

I dragged her out with blindfolds to spice her little sanity and aimed her with the gun only to scare her so that she would run as her life and that guy's life depended on it.

" Run,"

" Try to run from me again. try it, try it, try it, and I'll catch you again and again and again, I'll drag you back, strip you down, and remind you of to where and to whom your pretty little body belongs to."

Chapter 35

"Run,"

My conscious mind was yelling at me to do as he said. But I couldn't move a muscle. He had never played such a game before.

Something felt off.

"Bang!"

I screamed and fell backward on my bum. While still holding my hands against my ringing ears, I could smell the familiar smell of burn.

He missed huh. Not sure about the next time. Ughh. He was planning to kill me.

I had to run? Run?

I was now bare foot, quivering in this autumn breeze. Last time I attempted I literally was in full armour... Shoes and shit. Now I literally stood in my thin pajamas.

He circled me in a way he'd devour me. "I'll give you..." He stopped for a moment in contemplation before continuing. "An hour head start? If I don't catch you after half an hour, you win," he said.

An hour.

Where would I get in an hour? I had no idea how big the forest was, nor where I even was. I never tempted to step my foot in this enormous backyard. But how would this fair with no shoes on?

He whistled and sang his words. "You better run."

He didn't need to tell me twice.

I raced away, my feet being brutally charred by the rough, embattled earth beneath me. The icy mist from my own respiration engulfed my view as I climbed over the fallen tree trunk that blocked my path, the rough bark scraping mercilessly along my exposed thighs.

"Shit!"I attempted to remain quiet, but the searing pain that plagued the skin of my inner thighs made it challenging to maintain silence, for every little jostle aggravated the burn to the point that it was a torment to bear.

I wished I had worn underwear before going to bed.

I ran through the bushes that were as tall as me. The branches scratch me as I force my way in. It stung, it really fucking stung, but the pain, I knew would be tenfold if he got a hold of me.... Easily.

He would let me get away with spitting in his face if he had his wish fulfilled.This time was... The thrill of chase. In worst case scenario, I might end up with a bullet hole again.

He was unpredictable For sure. But not entirely a man with a bad temper. Temper? Bullshit. This fucked up man would literally stare at me sleeping for hours on end and slap me for making him wait when I hesitate to sit on his fucking lap.

For a moment I thought about giving up, letting him take me home and do whatever he wanted to do, it would take less energy that way.

Where the fuck do I hide?

Parts of the forest looked the same, it was a big bowl of trees, hills here, hills there, one big rock, another big rock, a stupid rope swing, a drizzle of water flowing downhill. It all looked the fucking same, what was I going to do?

I found a huge log and got inside as my feet were on fire. I tried not to make a sound but the freezing breeze wasn't helping me at all.

Even if I had to wait and hide here till the morning, I would. Losing one of his games was never a good thing. And Mateo's life was hanging on his hands.

Finally, I was calm, I sat down and curled into a ball in the log, gripping a handful of stones I found.

Tears were streaming down my cheeks again. That look on his face when he told me to run, it was ...the determination... of ending me???

Who was I talking about? He was a psychopath, he would kill me anytime he wanted, all he needed was an apparent reason. And I already gave him a reason to kill me by escaping.

I inhaled deeply and wiped my tears furiously.

Suddenly, I heard footsteps from afar. I froze... Not daring to breathe and I gripped the stone in my hand tighter.

But the footsteps were gone slowly. I gulped down slowly realizing my throat was dry from lack of air.

I slowly peeked outside, the place was dark but enough to see if someone was there. The silence was terrifying.

I decided I had to move forward. I didn't think I was safe in this log anymore. So I made myself ready to get up and run.

I closed my eyes and counted quietly. 'I'll step out and find a new place '

" Five,Four,...Three,...Two,-"

Before I could finish counting a pair of hands gripped my arms yanking me out."One," Damien whispered huskily into my ears.

I didn't think twice, screaming at the top of my lungs and swinging the stone to where his head was supposed to be.

His grip loosened with a groan, I sprinted away screamed bloody murder for help. Though I knew, nobody would hear me.

I could feel Damien was behind me as he was running after me too. How the hell did he find me so quickly???!!! I was sure I chose another direction.

I looked behind and saw his furious figure deadly close at my pace.

As almost I could barely step another two or three steps, my clumsy ass slipped, laying my tummy on dirty mud.

I flipped over and looked back at panting Damien...

Great Vivan...., now both you and Mateo are doomed...

He was also panting with his head down. I could see his temple was red with blood trickling from where I struck him earlier. I was heaving just like a fish out of water.

His heavy breaths were terrifying. Oh god. Don't let him torture me again. Just, just make him kill me quickly.

I stared at him as he kept his gaze on the ground with his palms on his knees. I was pretty sure he got an inner battle to calm himself.

Finally, he gazed at me. As soon as his eyes met mine, his furious expression was gone.

With an unknown expression, he kept staring at me. A couple of minutes passed he barely blinked.

Was that drooling? What was he? A feral animal? What the fuck was inherently wrong with this creepy chilling fuck-face?

But soon he slowly approached me...

That's it. I quickly shut my eyes and laid my head on the mud in relief. Finally, I was going to die. I was just tired. Maybe he would bathe me before burying me because I'm in desperate need of a shower...

Instead of unbearable pain or a loud gunshot, I felt his minty breath fanning my cheek.

I slowly opened my eyes meeting with his shiny grey eyes. I tried moving but everything was so heavy. But I didn't give up, I kept squirming. I could feel Damien's hands roaming around my body. Biting, Gripping and groping wherever he could touch.

He was murmuring something against my skin...

And just like that when I let out a particularly loud sob due to overwhelming touch and painful bites, his eyes returned that icy glare.

"If I weren't here, you would have died. Can't have that. I lied. I couldn't wait an hour. You're so pathetic, I had to make sure you didn't die out here. You lose, my doll."

I lost. No! No, I didn't lose, he cheated. I tried up and gripped at the loose dirt to get away, but I didn't get far, his hand was already gripped tight in my hair, pulling back to pin me where he wanted.

"Where are you going? I found you, remember?" He tugged so hard, it sent me crashing to the floor in a heap, he never let go of my hair. It burn so bad that I couldn't calm down.

I tried my hardest to claw at his hands, maybe that could have made him drop me, but his grip was unrelenting.

He pulled you up so I was on my knees, his fingers still wedged in the curls of my hair, my scalped burned like he could scalp me at any moment.

I struggled to open my eyes. Why was he doing this!? What did I ever do!!

When I felt something against my face, I braced for the soul sucking kiss but a strong chemical fragrance hit my nose.

He was holding a cloth against my nostrils. I wasn't able to hold my breath because it was so sudden.

My vision went blurry but it didn't knock me out straight away. I could feel my muscles relaxing... That was when I could feel him running his hand through my hair in soothing manner.

What the hell did he do to me??!!

A couple of minutes later, I"So beautiful," I heard Damien mumble as the last thing.

(detailed description from the view of psycho)

----------------------------------Damien Martin's POV

I freshen up and showered before starting my hunt.

Little did she know, I smirked and tracked down her location as I already put the tracker in her thigh. She was completely oblivious to that.

She was about 0.6 miles away at North.Hmmm. Smart girl. She changed the route and direction.

I knew that was cheating. But how was I supposed to find her this nightime in the forest? Also, I didn't want her to spend the night in the forest.

I would punish her in another way. The fun could wait.

I grabbed the chloroform bottle tugging it with the cloth. I didn't want her to waste her energies by struggling against me like the stubborn brat she was.

I checked my tracker, she was right in Infront of me.I looked around and saw a log.

I smirked and pretended to walk away. But I simply approached the log with light steps because I liked how helpless she was.

As I was near her, I could hear her fainted voice you would miss if you're not used to hearing it.

"Five,Four,...Three,...Two,-"

I didn't let her finish.I dragged her out and whispered into her ears," One,"

She screamed while struggling.But in a swift motion, a hard thing hit my head. I almost lost my balance as she shoved me back.

She used that opportunity and ran.'Oh, Vivan, you never learned,' All I see was red. I fucking hated that she still dared to raise her hand at me. The cornered prey always acted the same way that never failed to fuck my mood up. The violence in the face of power imbalance. Stupid and ignorant.

It didn't take me long to catch her.Instead, she slipped in the mud. I tried to calm myself down by looking down at the ground. I would surely hurt her if I looked at her right now.

I looked at her and my brain stopped working.

Her white gown was covered in mud mixing with her pale white skin, her long hair was partially on the ground and some strands stick her face with her sweat, her pinky plump lips parted slightly, her whole body shaking and she was heaving down, her beautiful slender legs were on show and her bare feet were red. All of her beauty was shining in the moonlight.

I was freaked out. How could a little girl become so gorgeous, right in front of my nose??? She was freaking beautiful!

Soft... Such a refreshing feeling. I could feel the curvature where her gravity of center was. Plump, handful, intoxicating even..I feel like I could mark it up or maybe devour it.

"Beautiful" I murmured the compliment from the bottom of my heart.

A sharp tug and a sound of something akin to desperation of wanting to GeTT the FuCk away from me.

A cry with that glossy eyes looking at me and telling me that I SuRe DoNt DeSeRvE HeR in any shape or form. Looking down on me? Challenging me? Trying to manipulate me?

"If I weren't here, you would have died. Can't have that. I lied. I couldn't wait an hour. You're so pathetic, I had to make sure you didn't die out here. You lose, my doll."

As expected she put up a fight and I was... Disappointed to say the least.

"Where are you going? I found you, remember?"

Hurt, Huh? Stuck up little bitch. Only if I could rid of this fleeting little existence from my life... But I sure as fuck could not think of a reason why I want to keep this little devil around.

I prepared to knock her out with chloroform.

I felt my stomach twisted looking at her beautiful body lying beneath me, still squirming since the drug took a while to work. I couldn't control myself anymore so I took in her beauty.

I touched her everywhere and her muscles were no where tense. As if she's asleep, but she's awake and... She's not ReSiStIng... Partly conscious... No pretentious facade ... Just... This little faint of a beating heart and glossy eyes shining with unshed tears.

"So beautiful," indeed.

Eventually, she stopped squirming and fell asleep with a steady breath.

My satisfaction was gone. I didn't like the fact she wasn't conscious while I was touching her. No response was just like her in a deep sleep. No fun.

I groaned and carried her back.Well, guessed I had to wait again...

"Being utterly vulnerable under my presence = embodiment of pure beauty."

ty."

'no notes author tired '

Chapter 36

(36)

I gained my consciousness only to encounter assault over my body.

My whole body was already aching and here, that bastard pressed me into bed and continued his assaults. He was hurting me...

I groaned and he seemed to notice that I was awake. He stopped and stared at me.

The effect of that chemical was coming down full force on me with a terrible headache. Then I remembered what happened. Was he going to kill Mateo? Or did he already kill him?

"Kiss me back now since you are awake now," I felt him tugging on my severely sore lips.

There was no point in making him angry more. I slowly sucked onto his lips and he remained unresponsive. I tugged harder at his bottom lip in frustration.

Very soon, he tugged my hair and hungrily kissed me back, making me forget whose air I was breathing.

He let me breathe for a while but attacked me again. I tried to push him this time because I could feel the burning sensation on my lips. How long has this been going? He was doing this intentionally!

He didn't even budge and pinched my arms to get me open my mouth again."It hurts-. Please-. S-stop-" He sucked harshly along my jaw and neck surely leaving marks, despite my pleas.

"Say that you're mine," he whispered.

" I'm yours," I answered quickly but earned a growl-like sound. What the hell did this bastard want?

He stopped what he was doing and cupped my face. "You know that you lose the game, hm?" He cooed as he put his forehead on mine.

I gulped down slowly and nodded. Smart-mouthing would not be the best for now.

"You do care for that fucker, don't you?" Damien said calmly. I could see his dilated pupils... Not good.

"I-I just d-don't want anyone to die," I shattered staring at his hypnotic eyes.

His eyes bored into mine. "But you lose the game," Damien said while brushing my face with the back of his hand.

"N-No! I mean, please... " I shattered. Oh, I was screwed.

He said nothing and started kissing along my collarbone. I learned that I was still in my dirty pajamas and felt the chill creeping up on me despite the room being fairly warm.

His lips stopped where the tattoo was.

"Did you like the tattoo?" He mumbled against my skin.

Ughh. There was no way out for that kind of question made by him. He would surely hurt me no matter what my answer was. He was making out a reason to hurt me.

So, I decided to say the truth," No, I hate that,"

" You lie," Damien whispered while kissing on the tattoo.

"You will hurt me anyways," I mumbled with a poker face.

He said nothing but stared at my swollen lips again. He quickly snapped his head after a couple of seconds. "I own you. I can do whatever I want with you," he stated licking on the tattoo.

I huffed in annoyance. He was more like a pain in the ass.

"You hate me, don't you?" his eyes back at my face. "And you hate the tattoo," he seethed. "

I didn't know what to say. He was in his own fucked up delusion. Interrupting his words would make it worse only. There was no way out. I had to suffer his wrath sooner. More like pent-up frustrations.

I gasped as Damien suddenly started sucking on my soft skin where the tattoo was. He even bit it.

I turned my head away from him and bit down my tongue preventing myself from crying out. Crying and pleading would only encourage him right now.

After he was satisfied, he pulled away. And I was a crying mess from the pain.

"Is it the design? Is it because of it being the two bold letters "D.M" ? Is it because how I tricked you into getting the tattoo which in case you absolutely have no rights to reject in the first place?!! Should I have used your official position of DAMIEN MARTIN'S LITTLE BITCH?!!"

I tried to hold my sobs in but failed miserably. What the actual fuck was wrong with this unstable piece of shit?!

"Maybe you don't like it because it might be mistaken as 'Direct Message' ? No pun intended though," his smile was of that uncanny vibe.

Twisted.

He suddenly yanked me by my hair and gripped my chin. "Do you like the tattoo or not???!!!" He yelled at my face.

"Yes, I liked it. Okay?!" I cried out.

He practically dragged me out of the room into the basement again. I was whimpering as my body was on fire.

He threw me into the basement again.I looked up at Mateo who was still breathing slowly in the position as I left him. Being tied into the chair.

And when my vision finally cleared, that's when I realised it was not Mateo... Just someone with a similar features.

"Yes? You say yes? Then, why did you tempted to leave me??!!" Damien stood near my laying form and yelled towering over me.

He pulled out the gun in a swift motion and put the tip on the guy's temple making my eyes widen in fear."With this fucker?" He seethed and unlocked the safety ready to shoot him.

" I-I" I shattered.

"Say it!! Admit it you care for this fucker," he furiously yelled at me.

"I-I do not care for him,-" I was cut off by a bang.

Did he shoot this poor guy dead? No, but the guys thigh was now bleeding profusely. I covered my ears and cried out scooting away from both of them. The guy was whimpering.

"Tell me a good fucking reason not to kill this smut," Damien seethed.

" P-PLEASE, I'm sorry. Don't kill him. Please ..." I sobbed. This was too much for me. On top of being scared I was bawling my eyes out. All the familiar feelings of being trapped and helpless weighing down on me while I hyperventilated.

Damien walked towards me and pushed me into the wall further, " What will I get in return, my doll?"

That's it. I knew it. He was playing the game to trap me with my own words.

"W-What do y-you want?" I sobbed.

" Just a favor," he answered back excitedly.

I looked at him and saw the sadistic and psychotic glints in his eyes. He tugged away from the gun and instantly pulled me gently to get up and carried me upstairs as if nothing happened a moment ago.

He made me sit on the bed and kneeled in front of me. The intensity of his gaze making me want to kick him in the face but I knew better. I took a long heave of breath at him kissing my knuckles softly.And replacing the feeling of his lips with a cloth.

I looked down at the silky plush of cloth he pushed into my hands.

" I'll give you ten minutes to calm down and I want you to come out with this."

I got up shakily and changed into that fancy dress in the wardrobe. A lingerie??? The length was way too short... I walked out uncomfortably, Damien was sitting on the couch leaning his back completely.

He had already closed the lights and only left the dim lamp-light open.

I couldn't see the expression in his face. The next three words he said made me froze.

"Strip for me,"

Chapter 37 (1) 16+

- -

3 ⁷ (1) 16+

Contain sensitive parts

Proceed with caution

"Strip for me," Damien's words pulled me back to reality. I literally just stood there with a blank head. I might be stupid sometimes, but not stupid enough not to get the hidden message behind it.

I could see the seriousness on his face.I slowly backed away earning a sharp look from Damien.

"I- I- can't," I stated.

He tilted his head upwards and leaned backward releasing his deep breath. As if he's tired of ordering a bad dog to sit down.

"You can strip by yourself or.. I can rip that apart from you and.. do something I will regret," he mumbled with a bored tone gazing at the ceiling.

His attention was slowly back on me licking his lips, spreading his legs, and slowly unbuttoning his shirt, as I stood stiffly, wishing he would forget I was in this room.

My head felt light but I couldn't even move a muscle. My reaction earned a raised brow, " Don't tempt me, we both know how my self-control is... ," He paused as his stare landed on my lips, and his gaze back to my eyes, " I just can't help it,"

He's lunatic enough to stare me in my sleep though the night. Everything about him was unpredictable. There could be times when I could spit and him and earn a smirk. Or he would pounce on me just because I looked at him Wrong. Even in my slightest change of demeanor and not. Anything would trigger him to attack me in the line of his sight for no apparent reason at times.

But... how could I? Why was he acting like this?

I felt the back of my eyes burned.My face became as hot as hell.I felt my throat itching.There's a chance of him losing control... I didn't even wanna think about it.

" Don't. Cry," Damien said with a low tone.

I couldn't stop the tears.

Damien was dead serious about this.

"A-are you-" I couldn't find my Voice, " gonna-"

He cut me off " Vivan, strip. "

" Screw you, bastard! The hell I would strip for you! " I blurted out. Realising I just snapped at him, I remained frozen, unable to move from my spot.

But I could feel his eyes looking me up and down. He looked as if he was trying memorize every part of me, I couldn't help but shiver as I thought of every possible outcome.

He hadn't reacted to what I just said.

I watched as he made his way over to me, in no hurry. He moved slow until he had me pressed against the wall. Caging me between his outstretched arms.

Maintaining eye contact was nothing but pathetic attempt to not show fear. But it was too much. The look in his eye was too intense. A lump form in my throat and my eyes began to tear up as his breath mix with mine.

" Vivan... Do you understand your place in this whatever relationship we have? "

" Please... I don't want to. "

"If you take it off on your own. I won't touch you. I can't give you the same promise if you Force my hand. Get it? "

His face moved into the crook of my neck, getting as close as he could without touching.

" Well?" He said calmly.

I took in a deep breath letting the frustrated tears fell and started pulling the dress off me with eyes closed tight.

" Doll, s-l-o-w-l-y,"

I was done taking off top leaving my chest bare with the fancy bra he made me put on earlier. It wasn't the first time he brought clothes for me to wear but it had always been in different situations. Especially not the situations where he demand to humiliate me by making me strip.

I peeked at him and he was back in his chair with eyes trained on me.

Now I was only in my undergarments.And the floor started to look extremely interesting. The light in the room was really dull with a single lamp across me right behind where Damien was sat.

I couldnt exactly make out his facial expressions. But the good thing was he might not even see me clearly in this lighting.

"Well, keep going, don't keep me waiting. "

There were times I had been fully naked in front of him whereas he walked in on me while I was showering and he didn't bat an eye. One of the rare moments of him completely ignoring me. Or else he would demand my full undivided attention on me. I figured he was a narcissist from the start.

I started unclasping the hook of the bra but Damien got up and walked towards me in a swift motion.

I was startled and stood still with my hands clutched in front of me as I was afraid of the consequences of backing away from him.

A hand met my throat bruisingly and another landed a harsh grip on my butt, not in a way that's hurting me but in securing me from moving.

"Do you hate me?" I swear I could see his eyes shining from tears. My imagination?

Great, Vivan. What are you gonna answer now?

" What if I say 'yes'? And what if I say ' no'?" I said staring at his face.

" There will be different consequences according to your answer," I felt him tightening his grip a little. An unspoken threat. A reminder.

I remained silent and he started unclasping my bra on his own.

My hands automatically reached out to my chest, covering it from his sinful stare.Damien said nothing but back away from me slowly never leaving his eyes on me.

I stood there emotionless.

I could feel his burning gaze on my body.

I heard him going through the drawer to take something out... A belt? No...

But a whip like thing.

I met his eyes where they twinkle with unknown glint before his hands go over to turn the lamp off leaving the room in pitch darkness.

But the moonlight fell upon into the room from the balcony. It was full moon day.

" Get on the bed and lay down. " he mumbled.

I felt my throat tightened with how much I was holding back from crying and throwing up. All the memories from that... particular night had me on chokehold as I shook my head in denial.

He couldn't be serious... He couldn't be seriously thinking about beating me with that thing when I had done nothing wrong.

Yeah. What did I do wrong? I did what he asked. I... I ran through the forest... I hadn't done anything wrong to make him mad. I hadn't cross any lines... Was that something I said... I called me bastard earlier... But he would have reacted right? Right? He couldn't... He wouldn't.

Not without Apparent reason.

" Damien, I .. I did nothing wrong. I did what you asked.. and and I'm really tired and I just wanted to go to sleep earlier and that's why I was being bitchy. It wasn't intentional, my legs really hurt just standing here. But please. You know I hate 'the belt' please. You're not.. going to... Right? Right? "

My words just bubbled up as I plead into the dark silluette in the corner of the room.

I heard the thing being dropped onto the floor. " Get on the bed now, "

I couldn't see him and sure as fuck I didn't want to know what he was planning.

I practically jumped onto the bed before he change his mind and pick up that curse tool again. I didn't realize I was shaking until Damien put the thin sheet on me.

He tried to pry my hands off my chest but I resisted.

" Doll," a particular harsh threat was all it took.

I relaxed and gave up. I sniffed and sobbed, gripping the pillow tightly.I hoped he would make it quick, as I waited for the whip to strike my flesh.

Minutes passed but nothing happened, so I fluttered my eyes opened and found grey eyes passionate but filled with lust.

He was kneeling on the bed while staring at me like the creep he was.

But soon, he started taking off his clothes. And I mentally cussed him out as he slowly crept under the bed cover.

The only thing that was covering me was a white sheet he gave me. But it wasn't helping at all, everything was on display.

I felt him breathing down my shoulder as he snuggled against me.

" Please..no. "

I felt him hovering over me as his eyes tracing the tears falling down my face. The position I was trapped in wasn't making it easy for me to see his face.

" What are you saying no to? What did you think I would do huh? " A particular mock tone had me biting back my tongue from saying something sour back.

"I wasn't planning whatever you think would happen," he whispered and peeled off the cover from me making me completely expose.

My eyes widened in pure fear.

He pulled down his boxer making me turned away instantly.

What the hell was he planning????!!!!

His gaze went between our bodies and his smile widened. Looking me in the eye before he moved his face closer to mine.

He growled and gripped my chin,

" Look at me,"

I opened my eyes and regretted it, he was holding the h-his long, veiny thing.

I cried out like a banshee before trying to land a hit on his stupid face. I started screaming that I didn't believe him.

A hand tangled in my hair and light slaps bring me back to his manic laughing face. " You really are something, do you even have a clear idea of what you think is going to happen to you? "

Did he think I'm stupid? Of course I bet that's something not in my favor!

He made me lay side way facing him. His hand was covering his hard length. Moving up and down gently.

"Don't look away." His grip tightened around himself, his breath stuttering.

My gaze went back, he might as well have had a hand tangled in my hair and had been forcing my eyes to where he wanted them.

Giving soft strokes to himself. His movements began to quicken, I watched his knuckles whiten as gripped himself harder.

I flinched as he suddenly leaned closer to my face. His palm coming up near my mouth.

"Spit on it doll. "

I looked at him, dumbfounded. Like spit?

"Spit on my palm, if you don't I am going to have to find something else to ease this friction."

I gathered enough spit to drop in his palm. He guided his palm closer to his thing. I watched his hand slid it up his shaft.

He suddenly grabbed my hands in his grip as he straddled me. His other hand never stopped stroking his thing.

His words stuttered as he picked up his pace.

"Good fucking doll." His moans reverberated throughout the room.

"My little fucking spit bitch, fucking hell." His head dropped back, and I watched as white liquid landed on my belly, up between my breasts.

I made a disgusted face at his satisfied grin. And soon I was met with lips sucking everywhere on my face. I felt him feeling my breasts and trying to smear the sticky liquid all over my stomach.

Humiliation overwhelmed me.I was disgusted and ashamed.

I felt him collapsing behind me and him pulling me until my back was against him. I felt him trying to pry my thighs open. His ragged breathing told me that he was now using friction between my thighs to get off. I felt my underwear becoming drenched and I couldn't understand the weird feeling between my legs.

His groans were mixing with my sobs.

This was pure hell. I tried to struggle but he seemed unfocused as he kept pushing his thing between my thighs. It was all slippery on my thighs.

I grabbed on the sheet and buried my face in my palms waiting for this hell to end.

After it felt like forever, he growled loudly and I felt warm liquids dripping my thighs.

I shivered from the feeling of wet towel was placed between my legs.All I knew was wanting to shower.His hand gripping my thighs as I tried to get away from him.

" Don't move, sleep, I'll clean you up. "

I felt dizzy as I tried to push his wandering hands away.

" I'll take care of you, Like I Always Do... My Doll. "

www.ingramcontent.com/pod-product-compliance
Lightning Source LLC
Chambersburg PA
CBHW070337200726
48294CB00003B/694